INNOCENT IN THE
SHEIKH'S PALACE

INNOCENT IN THE SHEIKH'S PALACE

DANI COLLINS

MILLS & BOON

First published in Great Britain 2020
by Mills & Boon, an imprint of HarperCollins*Publishers*
1 London Bridge Street, London, SE1 9GF

www.harpercollins.co.uk

HarperCollins*Publishers*
1st Floor, Watermarque Building, Ringsend Road
Dublin 4, Ireland
Large Print edition 2021

© 2020 Dani Collins

ISBN: 978-0-263-28836-0

MIX
Paper from
responsible sources
FSC www.fsc.org   FSC C007454

This book is produced from independently certified
FSC™ paper to ensure responsible forest management. For
more information visit www.harpercollins.co.uk/green.

Printed and bound in Great Britain
by CPI Group (UK) Ltd, Croydon, CR0 4YY

For my editor, Megan Haslam,
who brought up some key points
when I pitched this book
(e.g. Make sure there aren't any
other stray samples!). And for you,
Dear Reader. Social isolation is my
normal, but it's so much easier to bear
knowing you're here with me
in these fantastic fictional worlds.

CHAPTER ONE

DRIVING IN NEW YORK WAS, hands down, worse than taking the subway, even on a Sunday. Hannah Meeks hadn't had much choice, though. She had come straight from a weekend research trip upstate and the clinic had been adamant she arrive by ten, offering to send a car for her if she couldn't get there on her own steam. They'd even given her a special code to open the gate to their private lot, promising her a spot.

None of that was a win when she had to be outside at all. Today was the sort of weather her grandmother would have said was "great if you're a duck." Ducks weren't dumb enough to be gadding about in this, though. Only her.

Hannah couldn't imagine what the emergency was. She'd paid all of her instalments on time and her pregnancy was progressing without hiccups. Well, a few actual hiccups on the baby's part, which she'd been assured were normal.

She punched in her code and nearly froze her hand off. The rain was turning to sleet, bogging down her wipers as she entered the mostly deserted parking lot. The drive to her small walk-up would be even worse, and she would need every type of good luck charm to find a parking spot within a six-block radius.

Maybe they would let her leave her car here for the night, not that walking to the subway station would be a picnic, either.

She sighed as she carefully turned her car's nose into a spot to the right of the entrance steps. Her sedan fishtailed as she touched the brakes, leaving her car at an angle that probably took up two stalls. She didn't bother trying to fix it. Frankly, she needed the extra space to open her door all the way. Her belly had her sitting so far back from the wheel that she could barely touch the pedals.

Checking her reflection, she heaved another sigh. She rarely wore makeup and had a few more months before her adult braces could be switched for a retainer. Why had she thought this pixie cut was a good idea, though? Her hair had just enough curl that the little wisps turned up on the ends, especially where they landed against the frames of her glasses. No matter how she smoothed the front, her bangs sat crooked. She looked like a six-year-old who had cut her own hair with garden shears, then put on her grandfather's horn-rims.

She jammed her hat on, pulled on her gloves, buttoned her coat and gathered her phone and keys into her bag. Her windows were starting to fog, and when she tried to open her door, she found it had—seriously?—frozen shut! Well, now what?

She dug into her bag for her phone, thinking to call into the clinic for assistance, but just then, an SUV pulled in a few spaces over. A man leaped out of the passenger seat and popped open an umbrella before he opened the back door for another man.

The door was slammed, and the men would have hurried into the clinic, but she snapped to her senses and gave her horn an urgent series of toots, then squeakily rubbed a hole into the foggy window beside her.

"Help! Excuse me! Can you help, please?"

She heard one ask a question in a language that might have been Arabic. They wore woolen overcoats and their heads weren't covered, but they both had dark skin, black hair and closely trimmed beards.

"I need help!" she shouted louder as they stood there. "My door is frozen."

And I'm going to need a powder room ten minutes ago. Panic stations, gents.

The one with the umbrella grumbled something, but the other impatiently took it. It was useless anyway. A gust of wind drove the sleet sideways, turning the umbrella inside out. He shoved it back at the other man and came to glower at her through the little circle she'd made in the fogged glass.

Her heart leaped in surprise, alarm, fear. Maybe a hint of desire?

He was a blurred impression of height and intimidation, thirtyish, and good-looking despite his frown. His overcoat gaped and showed a dark blue suit that appeared to be tailored and probably was. The clinic catered to the supremely wealthy. She was very much a charity case who'd got in on a *who-you-know*, after doing a huge favor for the head administrator's wife.

"What are you shouting about?" he demanded.

"My doors are frozen. I'm stuck!" She demonstrated by trying the latch and giving the door a shove with her shoulder.

He frowned and tried it himself. Then he circled her car, trying all the doors with enough force to make the car rock. None opened.

He said something to the man trying to fix the umbrella. A third man emerged from the SUV while the first came back to her window and asked, "You're sure it's unlocked?"

Oh, dear God. She wanted to die then. She pressed the button and heard it release.

Her would-be knight yanked opened the door to let in an icy blast—and that was just off his thunderstruck expression.

"I am *so* sorry." Had he ever heard of pregnancy brain? "I forgot that I hit the locks when I came into the city. You never know when a carjacker will try to jump into your car at a stop light, you know?"

He did not know. He *dared* carjackers to even think about looking in his direction. He continued to glare at her with exasperated disgust while the wind tried to tousle his short, thick hair. Silly wind. Nothing tousled him. He thrust out a hand, glance hitting her belly as she twisted to get her feet onto the ground.

"I can manage," she lied, feeling even more ridiculous as she tried to shoulder her bag and search out a safe place for a firm grip while the parking lot looked to be an ice rink.

"Can you?" he asked with scathing sarcasm. "Give me your hand. I'm not going to be responsible for a woman in your condition slipping and falling."

"Thank you." She begrudgingly took his hand and her heart leaped again, this time with a sharper, higher skip and a resounding thump as it landed back in her chest.

She had expected his palm to be smooth, but his grip was calloused and incredibly strong, making her feel ultrafeminine even as she heaved herself out of the low car with the grace of a baby hippo. She tried a nervous smile, but he was the furthest thing from interested in anything beyond getting her into the clinic and out of his un-tousled hair.

All three of the men were swarthy and handsome, wearing expensive overcoats and deadpan expressions. But the one who had helped her seemed to be in charge. While he held her hand, the other two made themselves busy. The guy with the umbrella rushed to close her door and steady her other elbow, and the third man raced ahead to trigger the automatic doors as Hannah kept a waddling pace across the slippery sidewalk and up the snow-caked steps.

"This is very heroic of you, thank you," she said, gripping her rescuer's firm arm.

The umbrella-holder followed behind them, trying really hard to keep the umbrella over his partner, but it was moot. They were all soaked and her dark knight in woolen armor spoke impatiently again in Arabic, brushing him off.

They stepped through the first set of doors

and she sighed with relief as they all wiped their feet on the mat. She hurried through the second set of doors, past the reception desk, blurting, "Hannah Meeks" as she headed straight into the powder room she had used on previous visits.

A few minutes later, considerably more comfortable, she tried again to do something with her reflection. It was a lost cause. Her hair now had a dose of static thanks to her hat. Fine brown strands stood straight up, making a halo around her red-nosed face.

Hopefully, she wouldn't have to face her rescuer in the waiting room. If she did, perhaps she could smooth things over by offering to take on any urgent research projects he might have. It was basically her only marketable skill beyond her paid position as a university librarian, but it had come in handy with the making of junior here. But who was her savior? And who were the other two men he was with? It seemed like they could be his bodyguards. With those signs of wealth, it definitely fit that he might need protection, but why was he coming to a fertility clinic without his partner?

Making a donation? She snickered into her hand at her own pun and decided to quit speculating about him since he'd likely already forgotten about her. She was extremely forgettable, as she had been reminded as recently as a year ago, when she'd bumped into the young man who'd taken her virginity her freshman year of college. He'd stared at her blankly, flummoxed that she'd greeted him by name. Humiliated, she had wound up lying and saying they'd met at a faculty event.

Ignoring the scorch that arrived against the back of her heart, she tugged her thick brown pullover down her belly, as if that would change anything. The knit bounced right back up, revealing the plain black camisole she wore tucked into the stretchy panel of her maternity jeans. So classy.

Hannah was not one of those women who glowed through pregnancy while transporting a cantaloupe behind their belly button. Nope. Her front was as big as one of those giant yoga balls some of her colleagues sat on at their desks. Her butt was wide as a delivery truck while her breasts had barely grown a cup size. She was the opposite of a figure eight—an egg. She still wore her hiking boots—having visited Grammy's resting place before driving back to the city—and the shoes that were good for tramping through the cemetery reading gravestones didn't exactly lend grace or comportment.

It's a girl, her grandmother would have said. *Girls steal their mother's beauty.*

Hannah gave a wistful sigh at Grammy not being here to meet her great-grandchild, but she doubted Grammy would have approved of Hannah's method of conception.

At twenty-five, Hannah had quit waiting for Prince Charming. She had never had any beauty to be stolen. Boys had been cruel, and men forgot her. Even women failed to notice her enough to ask, *Can I help you find a size?*

Hannah was that dreary cliché: a spinster librarian. But she had recently taken her future into her own hands. She had always known she wanted a family. She was confident her child wouldn't care if she had crooked teeth and freckled skin, a few extra pounds and a tendency to sniffle her way through allergy season. Being a single mother wouldn't be easy, but it would be easier than being alone.

For the first time in her life, she was optimistic for her future. Excited and confident. She refused to let anyone make her feel insecure about how she looked, even herself.

She quit fussing with her reflection and left the powder room. A nurse stood at the counter, waiting expectantly for her.

The Crown Prince of Baaqi, Sheikh Akin bin Raju bin Dagar Al-Sarraf, was trying not to allow the unthinkable into his head, but he didn't lead his country's military so successfully by failing to add up the evidence before him. In fact, his keen intelligence and ability to recognize and defuse small conflicts before they grew into wars was one of his greatest assets.

The facts he'd been gathering the last few days were foretelling only one disastrous, explosive outcome. It was a circumstance so infuriating that he cast about for any other explanation, but he instinctively knew he was wasting precious brain power and time.

A sperm sample was unaccounted for. An urgent meeting with the head administrator of the clinic had brought him from his father's sickroom. The nurse had insisted on waiting for the very pregnant woman toddling toward them to reappear before showing *both of them* into a meeting.

What a bizarre woman. She seemed utterly, cheerfully ignorant of the gravity they faced as she flashed a mouthful of metal and said, "Thank you again for your assistance."

His bodyguards had been alarmed by her honking and demand for assistance earlier. Akin, however, had instinctively known what he faced the instant he glanced at the lone woman arriving for an appointment on a day when the clinic was otherwise deserted. It wasn't a round of gunfire, but the next few minutes would tear gaping holes through his life. He knew it.

His second impression of her wasn't any more reassuring than his first. She had her overcoat over her arm but was still very bulky with heavy pregnancy. She had removed her hat to reveal an asymmetrical punk rock haircut that was the furthest thing from flattering. Her face was round and bare of makeup behind dark-rimmed glasses that turned her eyes into mousy brown beads. Her lips thinned into a self-conscious line as she succumbed to what he imagined was a habit of hiding her teeth.

"Hi, Hannah." The nurse's smile faltered as she swung her attention toward him. "Dr. Peters will see you now."

Hannah flashed Akin another oblivious smile as she swept past him.

Akin might be in deep denial, but that didn't stop him from taking every sensible precaution. He issued a few brief orders in Omid's direction.

Omid nodded and took out his phone.

When he fell into step behind her down the narrow hall, Hannah glanced over her shoulder with confusion and tried to see past Akin to the waiting room.

"Do you work here?"

"No," he said flatly.

"Then why—?"

"Here we are." The nurse knocked once and pushed into an office.

Dr. Peters rose and greeted them with a

tense, apprehensive nod. His balding head was shiny with perspiration. His hands nervously smoothed the lapels of his white coat. He started to come around to shake Akin's hand, but Akin stopped him with a flick of his wrist, silently telling him to skip the niceties.

"Your Royal Highness." The doctor bowed slightly. "Have you met Ms. Meeks?"

Ms., not Mrs. A small mercy? Akin's mind raced to the next steps in what he needed to do to recover from this ambush.

"Not officially. Hannah. And you're a Royal Highness?" Hannah's surprise was filled with confusion as she looked between them. When the door clicked closed behind the nurse, Hannah finally began to look concerned.

"Sheikh Akin Sarraf," he introduced himself, using his simplified English address to save the doctor bumbling through his full name. He and Hannah were about to become closely acquainted. No use standing on ceremony.

"The Crown Prince of Baaqi," the doctor impressed on Hannah.

"Am I, though?" Akin asked in a light tone that made generals shake in their boots.

The doctor went white.

"I don't understand why we're both here," Hannah said in bafflement, glancing warily at the closed door.

"You will. Have a seat," Akin said.

The doctor sank back into his own, hands trembling as he shifted a couple of file folders on his desk.

Hannah took the arms of a chair and lowered herself into it, but Akin remained on his feet, arms crossed, bracing himself for the bombs that would land in the next few seconds.

"I presume you found the misplaced sample?" he prompted.

"What sample?" Hannah blurted, snapping her head around and proving herself not completely lacking in the ability to make a deduction. Her hands took hold of the arms of her chair so tightly her knuckles went white. She leaned forward as though ready to leap back onto her feet.

Dr. Peters drew a shaken breath and sent a *deeply* remorseful look toward Akin that did not move him one iota. The doctor swallowed.

"To bring you up to speed, Ms. Meeks, I should tell you that Sheikh Akin's brother—"

"The late Crown Prince," Akin interjected.

"Yes. Um… Crown Prince Eijaz was a client. Sadly, he succumbed to a lengthy battle with cancer in March. Before he began his treatments, he had us store six sperm samples, in hopes he would survive and marry. He wanted to ensure he could produce an heir."

Why Eijaz had chosen a New York clinic would remain a mystery. He had been diagnosed while visiting here, so it might have been an impulse or convenience. The clinic had an excellent reputation, but it was clearly not infallible.

"I'm very sorry for your loss," Hannah said, sounding sincere. "But I'm sure that news has nothing to do with me." She spoke firmly, rejecting the obvious conclusion the way Akin had fruitlessly tried to do. She was pushing her whole body deep into that chair now, shoulders rounding defensively, hunkering down for the inevitable that she could sense was about to befall her.

"The royal family recently made the difficult decision to destroy the Prince's samples. Prince Akin is—" the doctor cleared his throat "—*currently* the acknowledged heir."

At no time had Akin coveted that role, despite all his father's failings and his brother's glaring lack of capacity for ruling a country. Akin had long moved past any opinions whatsoever on being "the spare." He had no feelings beyond grief at being called upon to take up the duties of king.

He had begun to prepare for the responsibility, though.

And now he was being relegated to the shadows again. It wasn't that it stung; it was just so damned cold there. Bleak.

Hannah was looking at him with a small frown, as though she could see past his hardened expression into the turmoil he worked so hard to ignore.

"In the course of our task, it was discovered we only had five of the Prince's samples in our bank," Dr. Peters continued.

Hannah brought her attention back to him. Her color had been leaching from her skin through the last minutes. She licked her lips and spoke in a voice that was very careful, as though she was fighting to hold on to her composure.

"Are you asking me to bring my dogged librarian skills to bear and help you find it?"

"Please, Ms. Meeks. Let's not have jokes. This is an extremely serious matter." The doctor shot Akin a look that was downright terrified. "We had the blood sample you donated last month for our research database. We used it to run a DNA test and can confirm that Prince Eijaz's sample was used to inseminate you. I'm very sorry."

Akin had been expecting exactly this, but it still punched a curse from his lips. The profanity rang loud and clear in the small room. He didn't apologize. His brain was folding in on itself with the ramifications. He began formulating his best plans of action, seeking a win while protecting his flanks.

Hannah only gave a disbelieving huff.

"You're sorry? Why? I didn't know the do-nor's name and now I do. That will be nice if any health concerns arise in future, but nothing changes. I have the baby I wanted and I'm the furthest thing from sorry for it."

Akin had to admire her bravado. It wasn't true confidence. Her voice quivered. Behind that poise, she understood that reality as she knew it had been altered irrevocably, but she was pretending she still had choices. Autonomy. If he was a man with a heart in the metaphoric sense, he might have found it endearing and called her "cute" for it.

"When are you due?" Akin asked her.

She jolted. He realized he was using the tone that snapped young soldiers into following orders.

Not a single enlisted man would dare refuse to answer him, but she stubbornly set her jaw and sealed her lips, as though refusing to speak would somehow help her keep that baby all to herself.

"Six weeks," Dr. Peters provided after a glance into one of the files before him. "December 29. The sex is…a boy. Congratulations." He threw a smile toward Hannah. "Everything is progressing normally."

"What the *hell* are you doing? *I'm* your patient," Hannah interjected with a tap against her breastbone. "I don't know him." She pointed at Akin. "I did not give you permission to share my confidential information. *I* didn't even want to know the sex. Are you completely abandoning professionalism and embracing full clown car?"

Apt description, and Akin empathized with her flare of temper. He really did. But he controlled his own as Dr. Peters continued to speak.

"We understand this is distressful and will be taking responsibility. Our lawyers have been notified and will be in touch to work out fair settlements with both of you."

"How charmingly American," Akin said tersely. "Throw lawyers and money at a problem to make it go away." The clinic would suffer a higher premium on their future malpractice insurance, but otherwise remain unscathed. If anything, their reputation would benefit. Women would line up for a chance at accidentally carrying royal blood. Whatever was awarded to Akin's family would be a drop in the bucket of billions they already possessed and would provide no real compensation for all that was about to happen.

Because he and Hannah faced a lifetime of reckoning with this error.

"It doesn't matter how this happened, since it *has*, but how did it?" Akin asked.

"We had a flu sweep through the clinic. Hannah's doctor was sick along with other key staff. Once a woman has prepared for the procedure, we don't like to ask her to wait. We're very tightly booked and had an intern—"

"I get the picture," Akin cut in, already bored with the perfect storm of incompetence.

"Whether I'm awarded a settlement or not, I intend to continue paying my instalments." Hannah set trembling fingers atop her bump. "So there's no question this baby is completely mine."

So cute. Truly.

"Is she safe to travel?" Akin asked.

"If the appropriate precautions are taken." The doctor used a handkerchief to dab the beads of sweat from his brow as he glanced at Hannah. "I have a nurse standing by to accompany you."

"To go where?" Hannah pinched her arm. "Am I even awake? Did I slip on the ice and I'm in a coma?"

"Hannah, the Sarraf family is very wealthy and powerful. I recommend you cooperate—" the doctor began, but she cut him off.

"No," she said resolutely. She flattened her feet to the floor and thrust her belly into the air as she pushed herself to stand. "I don't care what your inept intern did or how formidable your deceased client's family is. This is *my* baby. Not *yours* to give away to someone else. Definitely not *his.* I'm going home. I will drink my cup of chamomile tea and have a nap. When I wake up, I will discover this didn't even happen."

"Prince Eijaz didn't approve this use of his sperm," Dr. Peters said in an urgent effort to reason with her. "If you weren't so far along, we would insist on termination—"

"Don't you *even.*" Hannah had one hand splayed on her belly. She slapped the other onto the doctor's desk, looking as though she would vault over it and tear out the man's throat. Her face turned red. Her expression was the most threatening thing Akin had ever seen on a woman. It was a sight to behold and he had to respect her for it.

"The doctor is wrong," Akin interjected. "Termination would *not* be an option. Your son is the next ruler of Baaqi. That wouldn't change no matter what stage of pregnancy you were in. I would die protecting his life, today or any other day, as is my honor and duty."

Hannah straightened and looked at him with confused mistrust. "That won't be necessary."

"You don't know that, Ms. Meeks," he said with dry irony. "The future is extremely unpredictable, as our present circumstance demonstrates. Neither of us expected this would be our destiny an hour ago, did we?"

"My destiny hasn't changed."

"It very much has," he informed, experiencing an uncharacteristic shred of pity. He might have spared some for himself if he didn't know what a useless emotion it really was. "Our rulers are born in Baaqi, Ms. Meeks. Therefore, you are coming with me. You may stay as our guest and provide the loving care and guidance you clearly intended to bestow on him as he grows up there, but that is where he will grow up."

"*Counteroffer.* You ask Dr. Peters for a referral to a psychiatrist, because you're clearly delusional. Goodbye."

CHAPTER TWO

HANNAH WAS SHAKING so hard she could barely walk. She had to set a hand on the wall as she made her way down the hall, feet heavy as lead while her heart raced, and her vision going in and out.

It didn't matter who the father was. That was the conclusion she had reached when she had decided to seek artificial insemination. All she'd wanted was a healthy specimen and she had been assured she had one.

She had been *happy* not knowing who the father was. It meant the baby was all hers. There wouldn't be any troublesome interference from a deadbeat father or an interfering mother-in-law. She had had a very special relationship with her grandmother, and she had looked forward to that same unconditional embrace of familial love. The kind that made a home a home. That made life worth living.

Dear God. The umbrella guy from the SUV had replicated into six more. They were all dressed in flawless dark gray suits with black-and-silver striped ties. One melted through the exit when she appeared. The pair stationed at the door each set out a hand to indicate she couldn't pass. Two more stood next to the only other doors that led from the reception area. They all looked past her as she appeared.

Because the prince, or sheikh, or whatever Akin was, had practically stepped on her heels the whole way down the hall. She refused to look at him as she shrugged into her coat, but it didn't change the fact her heart was hammering so loudly it threatened to knock her over. Or that she felt his presence looming like a cloud that would envelop and smother her.

"Ms. Meeks will be traveling to Baaqi with us. She will be shown every consideration." He didn't touch her but halted close enough behind her shoulder that she felt the warmth off his body, even through her coat.

"I'm not getting on a plane with you!" Hannah looked to the reception desk, but the waiting area was deserted. What the *hell*? She thought about shoving her elbow into Akin's gut and making a run for it—as if his rugby team of bodyguards wouldn't tackle her.

"Give your keys and address to Omid. He'll ensure your things are forwarded."

His voice had the most authoritative ring of *Do it* she'd ever heard, but she had a lifetime's experience of standing up to chauvinists, misogynists and bullies. She straightened her spine—which only stuck her belly out further—and bluffed a complete lack of intimidation.

"No." What was he going to do? Beat her up and risk this precious baby he was sworn to protect?

"Hannah." Along with the musical lilt intrinsic to his own language, his English held a crisp British pronunciation, as though he'd learned it at a fancy boarding school. It added an annoying note of condescension to his air of superiority. "You're a vulnerable woman who is heavily pregnant. You've just received very shocking news, so I'm over-looking your insolence, but don't mistake my patience for weakness. You have arrived at the limit I possess. If you want a power struggle, we can engage in one. I will win. That won't be good for any of us, most especially the baby."

"What am I supposed to do? Defer to whatever you decree?" She waved a wild hand.

"Most people do. It makes everything run more smoothly."

The arrogant ass wasn't even joking.

"Let's speak somewhere with more privacy," he suggested.

She didn't move, aware in the back of her head that, much as she wanted to, she couldn't pretend this wasn't happening. Tears of panic were hot behind her eyes, but she fought them just as she fought to remain rational. Surely they had options that didn't include overturning her life?

"You can follow me to my apartment." She turned and swept past his door guards but was pulled up short by the snow falling like clumps of mashed potatoes beyond the second set of doors.

One of the bodyguard clones stood in that soppy mess next to Akin's SUV, ready to open the door when his boss appeared.

"You can't drive in this." Akin arrived beside her. "Come with me. One of my men will take your car."

"I can drive myself. I drove here, didn't I?" She closed her lips over that. If he said one word about how she had locked herself in her own car...

"My vehicle is safer. My driver is trained for inclement conditions. You already know I'm chivalrous. I helped you out of your car and walked you in, didn't I?"

Worst mistake of her life, relying on him for five seconds.

"I'm not going to let you talk me into anything," she warned.

"But you do understand we've been put in a remarkable position. It needs further discussion." He offered his arm.

After a final moment of hesitation, she went outside with him, down the steps, and clumsily climbed into the back of his SUV.

He came in beside her and offered, "Seat

warmer?" He pressed a button, then held out his hand. "Keys."

It was a relief not to have to drive. She excavated her keys from her bag, letting him relay them out the door before she realized—"I need those to get into my apartment."

"They'll be there before we will."

The doors shut and the SUV pulled away. She pondered that comment, looking back to see two of the men climbing into her messy car, moving her laptop case into the back seat. But just as she began to fear she was being a complete ninny and had participated in her own kidnapping, one of the men in the front asked for her address and relayed it to the other men.

She relaxed a little and glanced at Akin. He was bringing his telephone to his ear, speaking in Arabic.

She could point to Baaqi on a map, but she didn't recall much about it beyond it being incredibly rich in oil reserves. It was one of those small lynchpin countries that had suffered unrest over the last decade, from both inside and along its borders. Everyone knew who Crown Prince Eijaz was, of

course, and not just because he was a pho-
togenic playboy with millions of online fol-
lowers, forever vacationing with beautiful
women while caught up in one sexy scandal
after another. No, he was notorious for his
petulant social media post a few years ago,
when he'd been stranded in the Maldives. It
had sparked a meme that was regularly re-
posted in response to tone-deaf First World
problems.

My avocado toast is scorched.
Oh, muffin. It's like the time your private
jet broke down in the Maldives.

She was having a hard time comprehend-
ing that *that* man had fathered her baby. It
didn't fit in her head that her baby's father
was an infamous philanderer and his brother
was...? She hadn't even realized there was
another Prince of Baaqi.

She pulled out her own phone to learn
more, but Akin reached out to cover her
screen.

"We'll keep this between us for now."

"I was only going to look something up."
Him. She dropped her phone into her bag.

It was nice, though, that he thought she
had the kind of friends whom she would text
Guess what just happened to me? She did
have people in her contacts list. She wasn't
the isolated child she had once been. These
days she had colleagues who were polite
enough to invite her to retirement parties
and baby showers. Students brought her a
latte when she saved their bacon by sourc-
ing a book or other reference document they
needed. She was friendly with some of the
authors she worked with, but only with the
sort of online chatting that was mostly super-
ficial. Do you have kids? No, but I want one.

Friendships had never been her strong
suit any more than suitors had. Growing up,
Hannah had had her grandmother to ease
the sting of friends turning on her or dropping away, but after Grammy passed and
she'd rented out their bungalow in Syracuse
to take her current job at Columbia University, loneliness had become her most stead-
fast companion.

That first year had been a backslide into

her worst self-denigration. When she had found herself alone in bed at the end of it, greeting the New Year by watching a classic rom-com for the millionth time, she had resolved to quit waiting for someone to want to spend the rest of his life with her and fall in love with herself instead.

She had made a list of all the things she wanted out of life, including nicer teeth. "Family" had topped it and she'd been ticking things off, one by one, slowly making her best life come true until—

Her best life *was* coming true, she assured herself, setting a hand on the side of her belly where a little foot was giving a restless nudge.

Akin said a final few words and ended his call, then spoke to her without inflection. "My parents are looking forward to meeting you."

That wasn't how it had sounded. She might not know how to swear in his language, but that had definitely been the gist in the other man's weak, gruff tone.

This was the moment to say something

pithy about them visiting New York in the winter, but he continued speaking.

"I presume you're unmarried, since no one came with you to the meeting. Do you have a partner who was expecting to help you raise this baby?"

She frowned, not liking his phrasing, as though he was saying that whoever might have expected such a thing could kiss that scenario goodbye. She had a brief impulse to claim she did, but his cool way of looking down his hawkish nose sent reverberations through her, warning her against making silly mistakes.

Besides, they were going to her apartment, where it was plain she lived alone.

"No," she replied.

"Family?"

"My mother died when I was young. My father wasn't in the picture and my grandmother raised me. She's also gone."

"What was your plan? What sort of work have you been doing?"

Again with the past tense. She deliberately answered as though her plans were unchanged. Her plans *were* unchanged, she insisted to herself.

"I'm a librarian at Columbia. I'm taking a year's leave of absence beginning at the end of this month. I'm going to Syracuse, to live in the house where I grew up. For the last few years, I've been building an online business doing research for authors. If that continues to go well, I may quit the university altogether and stay home until the baby starts school, but I haven't ruled out coming back to work here or taking a position at another library elsewhere. I like to have options."

"Don't we all," he said with an ironic curl of his lip that struck foreboding in her soul.

Which was when she realized they weren't anywhere near her apartment and were, in fact, crossing the bridge into New Jersey.

"You said we would meet your men at my apartment!"

"I said they would get there before we did. We are not going there."

"That's still a lie! Is that how we're doing this? Because I can lie, too. I haven't, but I'll start," she warned.

His cheeks went hollow. Otherwise he sat very still, hands resting on his thighs. After a moment, he nodded once. "Lying is counterproductive. You're right. I won't mislead you again."

"And I'm supposed to believe that as you kidnap me to… Where do you think you're taking me?"

"My private jet is waiting to fly us directly to Baaqi. I've arranged our own nurse. I can't trust anyone from that clinic. Our flight plan ensures we'll have suitable places to land should any emergencies arise."

"I was being facetious. This *is* a kidnapping!"

"It is."

She could only choke, too flabbergasted to find words.

"You asked me not to lie," he said without a hint of sarcasm or remorse.

"I asked you to take me home."

"I know." His hands made one restless stroke to his knees and returned to the middle of his long thighs. "I understand you want your life to carry on as normal, Hannah. It can't. You are carrying the next ruler of my country. My nephew. If you think that doesn't matter to me, you are deeply mistaken."

Everything about him was very stoic, but he had lost his brother recently, she recalled, then stamped down on any compassion that incited in her.

"I liked it better when you lied," she muttered.

"That ship has sailed."

She studied him, wondering if he really did feel some connection to this baby.

"You miss him? Your brother?" Maybe it was a test of his willingness to be honest. Would he crack and admit to such a human emotion?

"I do," he said after a very brief hesitation, sounding pensive. "But I don't wish to talk about him right now." He glanced at her. His expression was unreadable, but it was probably the most believable thing he could have said.

Impulsively, because she had been dying to share this with someone who might actually feel it as the stunning miracle it was, she picked up his hand and brought it toward her belly. "Was your brother a boxer? Feel what his son is doing to my kidneys."

Akin's hand tensed and he started to pull away.

It was probably overstepping royal protocol for her to touch him without permission. It was definitely unwise. There was something in the feel of his hand that made her bones melt and her head swim, but his gaze dropped to her bump. His brow flexed in a glimpse of agony and he let her set his hand in place.

"Wait for it." She kept one hand over his and used her other to press into the other side of her belly, coaxing the baby, "Don't be shy. Say hello to— *Oof.*"

His breath rushed out and his hand jerked away before he pressed it back into place. "Did that hurt?"

"Like an elbow on the subway," she joked, realizing he wouldn't have any experience with such things.

His brow remained creased and his gaze grew more absorbed as he looked at the roundness of her belly. He circled his thumb, soothing the spot where the baby had kicked.

No man had ever moved her, not in a sexual way. It was another reason she'd asked a clinic to help her make this baby. Akin's absent caress wasn't even meant to be erotic, but it awakened a sensual response in her, one that sent swirling tenderness through her while embarrassing her at the same time for having such a reaction.

"Do you…um…have a wife and children?" she asked.

"No." Maybe he heard some of her confused reaction in her voice, because he withdrew his touch. His cloak of distance returned. "Why did you want to have a baby alone?"

"I still do," she said pointedly.

He didn't move, but his stillness suggested thinning patience and made the air between them crackle with animosity.

Look at me, she wanted to say. *That's why I'm having a baby alone. No man wants me.*

She was horrendously aware of his staff in the front seat, who seemed to speak English, though. And it made her so *sad* that people cared more about how a person looked than who they were inside. She hated to admit she'd always been one of the people society rejected for no good reason at all.

When she answered, she kept her voice low, hoping only Akin could hear her.

"I dated when I first went to university, but relationships aren't all they're cracked up to be." Especially when so many young men had only been looking to score—sexually or on an exam—and cheating had been the goal in both exercises. "My grandmother was elderly and needed help, so I didn't have much time outside of school for socializing anyway. After she passed, I moved to the city and haven't connected with anyone, but I miss having family. The fact is, this pregnancy kind of fell into my lap. Ha-ha."

"How so?" He turned his head to regard her.

"One of my author clients is married to Dr. Peters. I made a joke one day that I wanted children but needed to find a husband first. She said maybe not and told me about the clinic. One thing led to another, and even though the clinic has a wait list and charge through the roof, I was given a consult and taken on as part of their research program.

I'm required to give occasional blood samples and answer health surveys for the rest of my life, but I'm happy to contribute to science, so…" She shrugged.

"The samples and questions will discontinue. My brother did not consent to being a research project and nor has my future king."

"Akin—may I call you that?"

"Of course."

She could have laughed at how accommodating he sounded when he was such a giant brick wall in every other way.

"I've decided to pick my battles with you. I'll let you have that one, so you'll be more inclined to compromise on really important issues. Like the fact I am not going to Baaqi."

"Do you know that I have spent more than a decade commanding armies, Hannah? Winning battles is my day job. Perhaps don't pick any with me."

She could have sobbed. She swallowed back her panic and sat straighter and tried to keep her head while fighting for her life with as much civility as she could muster.

"I have to fight you, Akin. Take a walk in this pregnant body of mine for a moment. Whatever you feel for this baby because he's a remnant of your brother, I feel a thousand-fold because he's a part of *me*."

"I understand that," he said politely and waited, but she didn't know what else to say, because she could already tell that whatever she came up with, he would counter and override. On the one hand, it was refreshing that he was willing to let her have her say before he told her she was only a lowly woman and should mind her place, but it still made her want to scream.

She huffed in despair and threw up a hand.

He gave a pained nod. "You begin to understand."

"No! I don't. No one has to *know* this was his sperm."

"*I* know. My parents know. *You* know. I would hope you understand that this baby has a birthright you don't have the right to withhold. What are you going to do? Wait until he's eighteen, then point to a spot on the map and say, *That's yours. Go rule it*?"

"Don't lecture me on my rights." The frustrated burn behind the backs of her eyes grew to near unbearable. She turned her attention to the view out the window, where a lack of tall buildings suggested they were nearing a private airfield.

She pressed her lips flat so they wouldn't tremble, but her voice still held a creak of emotion. "Once I decided to have a baby alone, I realized how much better that is. Simpler. I wouldn't be undermined by the other parent, wouldn't have to argue over which in-laws to spend Christmas with. I don't expect big things from my life. All I want is a little family. Me and my child, maybe a goldfish or a cat someday. It's unfair of you to say I'm asking too much by asking for that. I have a right to give my baby the life I planned. It's a good one."

"I don't disagree. For many it is. I envy you for having experienced such a simple life. But this is bigger than either of us, Hannah. This is where we both step up for the greater good of the baby."

"Oh?" she scoffed. "And what great sacrifice will you be making?"

"I'll be marrying a stranger, same as you.

I'm becoming a parent when it was the last thing I expected or prepared for."

"What? *No*." Adrenaline sent her hand shooting for the door latch.

He struck like a rattlesnake. His big body loomed over hers, pressing her into the seat while his hand encircled hers. He had caged her so quickly, it took her a moment to realize he was being incredibly gentle about it, even as she sensed his grip couldn't be broken and she had no hope of shifting the wall of his body so much as a fraction of an inch unless he wanted her to.

She panted in alarm, torso brushing his. He was very warm, his eyes like black coffee, the tip of his nose grazing hers as he held her stare. He smelled like spicy aftershave and snow and damp wool.

"I did say I will protect this baby, Hannah. Even from you, if it comes to that. Will you give me your word you won't do anything foolish?"

"No." She blinked hard to see him through a blur of angry tears. "We are *not* getting married. I am not marrying a stranger."

"It doesn't have to be forever, but our marriage will benefit the baby and—you'll have to forgive how cold-blooded this sounds—will help smooth things over in the press."

"That *is* horrible. All of this is!" She wriggled against him, trying to free her hand and only succeeded in feeling all the more ineffectual for it.

"This is reality, Hannah."

He held her for an extra second to prove the point that he was in charge, she was sure of it, because he waited until she settled before he gently brought her hand away from the door and set it into her lap. He settled back in his seat but continued to watch her closely.

"Our modern world can accept a woman having a baby out of wedlock. My people can even accept a monarch conceived with an unknown foreign woman. Both? That is a tough sell. More important..." His cheeks hollowed. "I trust I have your complete confidence?"

She snorted. "Who am I going to tell any of this to and be believed?"

"Fair point."

The SUV came to a stop near the stairs to

a sleek private jet. She dug her back deeper into her seat and clenched her hand around her seat belt, ready to fight being pried out of here and thrust onto that plane.

"Give us privacy," he said.

His men promptly left the vehicle to stand in the gathering dusk and falling snow.

"For health reasons, my father was about to abdicate to Eijaz before my brother's diagnosis made that impossible. My father's health has declined steadily since Eijaz's death. My mother is equally devastated by grief. We were waiting until after the anniversary of his passing before I officially took over from my father. Now…"

Akin's palm swept through the air in a far too subtle gesture toward the earthquake that had occurred a mere hour ago, altering both of their lives.

"Now what?" Her hands instinctively tightened further on the belt.

"Now I will rule as Regent," he continued without emotion. "Until my nephew is old enough to be crowned. Given that enormous responsibility and the influence I will have over your child, it would behoove you to be recognized as my partner. Otherwise you'll be dismissed as a paid surrogate and treated accordingly."

She gasped. "Don't you ever, *ever* suggest that I am some sort of brood mare that carried this baby for any reason except a very deep desire to have a child *of my own*. You don't have any rights to him. Do you understand that?" She was near shouting.

He was completely unaffected, and merely shook his head at her as though she was a recalcitrant toddler.

"What are you going to do, Hannah? You can't abdicate on your son's behalf. That's for him to decide eighteen years from now. How are you going to raise him 'normally' now? How are you going to raise him *securely*? Are you refusing to prepare him for the challenge of taking the crown? Tell me what you think the options are for any of us."

The bastard sat there with that patient, patronizing look on his face because he knew he had her. She didn't have any choice. Not really. She might receive a settlement from the clinic for this mistake, but it wouldn't match the resources he had at his disposal.

She would be lucky if all he did was drag her into court. She'd never had the pleasure of being sued, but she knew time was measured glacially in that forum and lawyers were obscenely expensive.

She had nowhere to go, so she escaped the only way she could. She buried her face in her hands. She was a smart woman, but no matter how hard she racked her brain, she came up with nothing. She couldn't even find anger. It was definitely there, simmering at the injustice of life and Akin's casual assumption of authority over her, but she had the rest of her life to wallow in bitterness over that familiar foe.

Right now, she had to fight for what self-government she could retain.

"I don't want to marry you."

"It's just a formality. We won't consummate it."

Oh, there was a surprise! She couldn't help her choke of hysterical laughter and was startled when something soft touched her hand. She lifted her head to see he was pressing a silk handkerchief on her.

"I'm not crying," she muttered, blowing

her nose into it. "I'm trying to keep my head from exploding. You don't want to marry me. Do you? Me," she stressed. "I am not a bride you would choose for yourself, am I?" It was a type of self-harm to spit it out like that, but she wouldn't delude herself into believing anything less.

His long silence was damning, but there was something in his hardened expression that made her think he was wrestling with his own demons behind that mask, not intentionally reinforcing hers.

"I have never enjoyed the luxury of choice when it comes to such things. The expectation has always been that my brother would made a selection from my mother's vetted short list of potential brides and produce an heir before I would do the same."

"That's pretty cold-blooded, isn't it? What about love or basic attraction?"

"This from the woman who chose the most dispassionate way possible to conceive her child? A successful marriage merges interests, not hearts." He somehow grew even more shuttered as he said that. "You and I share a common interest in someone who is of the utmost importance to both of us. Marriage is the best action for all of us."

"This isn't your baby."

"He's still my family."

"But…" She hesitated, then forced herself to say it because she had to know exactly how he envisioned things would be. "Don't you want children of your own?"

"We can discuss that at a later time, if you decide you'd like more children."

"And then what? Our marriage ceases to be platonic?"

"As we're both aware, the father is no longer required to be present when his children are conceived." He sent a sardonic glance to her belly.

"So you don't ever want to have sex with me," she said, speaking as plainly as she thought the situation warranted. "Are you going to have sex with other people? Are you gay?" she asked.

"Why would you think that? No, I am a straight man who has gone without sex for various lengths of time in the past. I'm capable of doing it again. Are you?"

"Yes." Duh. She was having a baby without having had sex, wasn't she?

"You planned to stay home and work at your online job. You can do that from Baaqi."

Not all of it. Sometimes she needed feet on the ground, but she could do a lot of it online and through correspondence to various library collections and other archives.

He was doing it; he was talking her into it! And she was already too exhausted to continue their war of wills to keep resisting his cutthroat logic.

"I can't just *leave*, Akin. I still have a few weeks of work—"

"It will be handled. My staff will close your apartment and ship your things within the week. Your employer will be notified." He was probably making all of that happen as they spoke, cutting all her ties to her old life, leaving her no path to go backward.

"What exactly will happen when I get there?" She hated herself for asking. It sounded too much like she was surrendering.

"We'll marry in a private ceremony, immediately. Then a single announcement will go out encompassing all of this. You needn't appear in public until after the baby is born."

"Every girl's dream." To be forced into a marriage that would be a paper-only footnote to bigger news, her existence hidden from view like a shameful secret. A brand sat against her heart, scoring deeper with each slighting word and potential action. "I don't want…" Her throat was so tight she could barely force any words out. "That. I don't want any of that."

"I know." Why did he have to sound so pitying? If he'd been outright mean, she might be able to hate him. That tone was far more cruel. It carried the same pained pitch Grammy had used when sharing hard truths. *Life isn't fair. We don't always get what we want.*

Hannah drew a breath, wanting to protest, but after a moment the air left her body in a rush. She deflated like a balloon, drooping forward, desolate but still refusing to cry. She had never missed Grammy more in her life.

"You will be well cared for, Hannah. Your child will have an incredible life."

"But it won't be *mine*." She sat up straight. Not her child. Not her life. "I won't ever forgive you for this, Akin."

He was only the messenger. She knew that. And he didn't look too bothered either way, but she was in agony because she knew what she faced would be hell. She had had to work really hard to find her confidence and turn the other "chipmunk cheek" to the incessant litany of insults that had come her way all her life. Bucky and Four-Eyes and Fats were the least offensive.

Now she would be in a new place, already a stranger who didn't know the language or customs. She might be educated and have basic manners, but she wasn't a polished diamond the way Akin and his family were. People like him didn't know what it was like to be someone like her. They didn't want to, not when they could point and laugh instead. Her suffering would have to be swallowed and endured, the way she'd done through each level of hell called "school."

And how would her son be treated if he

didn't come out looking look like some Botticelli cherub—

She snapped an accusing look at Akin.

"What?" he asked with caution, sensing the change in her.

No one would ever bully her child. *No one.* Not ever. Not without earning her unmitigated wrath.

Not that she knew how she would protect her son no matter which world they occupied, but being the mother of a future monarch would bestow a lot more power on her to quash attacks against her child. Her *son* would be less of a target, growing up in that role.

"If I go with you, I expect to sign a prenup that outlines clear and fair terms for our marriage and eventual divorce. It must include stringent language that declares my absolute right to oversee every single stage of his upbringing. If you agree to that—"

"I do."

"I'll hold you to that. No lies," she reminded, pointing her finger at him.

"You have my word."

"Fine." She reached for the latch again,

pausing to take in the red carpet that was collecting snowflakes as it trailed up the steps into the jet.

What on earth was she thinking?

But here he was, coming around and offering his arm to guide her into his world.

CHAPTER THREE

AKIN HAD THOUGHT Hannah was staging a sulk, setting her head against the window the minute she sat down, but she fell asleep before the plane left the tarmac.

A pang of something that might have been guilt or concern struck against the dented shell of honor he wore to shield against less tolerable states of mind.

She'd spoken briefly with the nurse when they'd boarded, but aside from a bit of breathlessness after climbing the stairs, he hadn't heard any concerns raised by either of them. If he had realized how tired she was, he would have sent her to the stateroom. He started to nudge her awake to do so, but she must be exhausted if she was crashing so hard and fast.

He waited until they'd leveled off, then signaled for a pillow and pressed the button to recline her seat. She barely stirred as he eased her from the window into a more comfortable position. He accepted the blanket from the attendant and draped it over her.

He tilted his own chair back alongside her, wishing sleep came as easily to him, but it never did. He felt as though he'd been on an adrenaline high for twenty years straight. It had grown worse, not better, as time passed.

He had chided Hannah that she couldn't expect to raise her son in America and have him ready to take over Baaqi at eighteen, which was true. Ironically, Akin wasn't much better prepared at thirty-two.

In his country—in his *family*—the first son was groomed for that role. Pampered and encouraged and revered. When not at school, Eijaz had sat with their father, learning the fine arts of diplomacy and protocol.

Akin had merely been an insurance policy, acknowledged as a member of the royal family but sidelined as expendable. When *he* was home from school, Akin had trained with the army, beginning with the foot soldiers at twelve. Nepotism had played little part in his rise through the ranks. He'd had to prove himself capable before he'd been given command of their forces.

Part of that stark contrast in treatment was due to the fact their father had once been challenged by his own younger brother for control of Baaqi. His father had not only become a hardened autocrat as a result, but he would brook no similar mutinies. He had made clear that Akin's value lay in his unquestioning loyalty toward his brother.

Akin had been devoted to Eijaz. For all of Eijaz's faults and sense of entitlement, he'd been the only one to truly care about Akin. Their mother had been broken by grief when Akin had been very young, and she'd developed a resentment toward him that was lately exacerbated by her eldest son's death and her declining mental health.

So Akin had suffered a constant message of inferiority as a child, but he had never begrudged his brother for his higher station. When their father's heart trouble was diagnosed, however, and the King had begun giving more responsibility to Eijaz, Akin had wondered if Eijaz's temperament was up to the task. The more money he was given to control, the less he controlled himself. Had drugs or mental health issues played a part? Akin couldn't say, but it had all come to a head two years ago when Eijaz had attempted to turn Baaqi into a beacon of modern ideals—something even their own father had opposed. The seismic political shifts had *not* made their country a darling in a part of the world that clung to its traditional values.

Akin had found himself in an impossible situation. The few times he attempted to discuss the matter, his father had accused him of dancing close to treason. His only choice had been to put out fires—often literal ones started by dissidents throwing Molotov cocktails.

He had dreaded what would happen when his father stepped down completely and Eijaz took the throne. That did not mean he had wished his brother dead, but a weight of guilt now cloaked him heavily for his doubts.

Eijaz's cancer had been aggressive and cruel. While his parents supported Eijaz, Akin had taken on even more responsibility. When the unthinkable had happened far more abruptly than they could absorb, they were all devastated, but there had been no time for Akin to grieve or ruminate or show any emotions. He had to prepare himself to take the throne. His father was weaker than anyone outside their need-to-know circle could imagine, and the stress of ruling was shortening the little time he had left.

Even so, the old man had spent what energy he had left on clinging to power, using that power to argue that Eijaz's sperm samples could be used to produce an heir. The logistics had been a blurry prospect. Could they ask a wellborn lady to conceive a future monarch without taking the baby's father as her husband? Did Baaqi want a ruler born to a stranger hired for the express purpose of carrying a child? What if conception was tried and failed? Then what?

After much discussion, his parents had resigned themselves to accepting Akin in the role for which he had been conceived—the fallback heir. He would produce their next monarch the old-fashioned way, via an arranged marriage with a woman of appropriate rank.

It had fallen to Akin to enact that difficult

decision. He had made the call to the clinic like a ruthless Shakespearean king, one who ensured his bloodline would not be threatened by his brother's issue. It had made him sick. Nothing about taking Eijaz's place felt good or right.

Within hours, the clinic had relayed the message that five samples were confirmed as destroyed. One was unaccounted for.

That had been three days ago, and he had known immediately that his loyalty to his brother was once again being tested. Nevertheless, Akin had rushed to New York to await the results of their prompt investigation.

Was Eijaz laughing, wherever he was? Because Akin had done the math. If Hannah was due at the end of December, she'd been inseminated shortly after Eijaz had passed. Akin didn't believe that those in the afterlife could reach into this world to shake things up, but this was definitely the sort of practical joke his brother would have laughed himself weak over.

Why Hannah, though?

Akin turned his head, studying her round,

pink cheeks. The way she was slumping, her chin had doubled and her glasses were sitting crooked. He gently removed them and set them aside, noting the frown she wore even when fast asleep.

Such a strange bird, so dull and brown and unassuming, but when provoked, her feathers ruffled up like she was ready to win a cockfight. She reminded him of the geese in the park next to his English boarding school. When they felt territorial, they wouldn't think twice about nipping someone's butt.

I don't want to marry you.

Like being goosed by a goose, her words had stung his ego more than doing real harm, but did she not know who he was? Even as second son to a king, women wanted him.

I am not a bride you would choose for yourself, am I?

A long-buried bitter agony had arisen in him when she said that. Although his mother had begun tracking potential brides for Eijaz and him even while they were still young boys, making note of social triumphs and bloodlines and dodged scandals, Akin had always been expected to wait until his brother had secured his own heir before Akin produced one of his own. The one time he'd thought to defy that expectation, he'd been quickly reeducated.

So he had dismissed marriage as a far-off thing, even when his mother's faculties began to fail. When he had affairs, he confined them to those times when he was outside Baaqi. He always ensured the woman in question understood their relationship was temporary. If she wasn't fine with that, they didn't progress beyond dinner, but most took him to their bed anyway. A prince was a catch, even if he only gave her bragging rights on a brief affair.

But future kings, apparently, were even more of a catch. Legions of eligible women had been reaching out since his brother's death, wanting to "check in" and offer "a quiet night in." He'd been exhausted with the courtship chase before it even started, but that didn't mean he wanted to marry tomorrow. Or to marry Hannah, a librarian who wore cheap pullovers and locked herself in her own car.

Why recalling that made laughter build in his throat, he didn't know. He'd been annoyed as hell when it happened. Delirium, he supposed. This had been a hell of a day, but for a moment his heart felt lighter than it had in a long, long time.

As was his habit, he cut short his straying thoughts and forced his mind back on task. He tried to anticipate all the possible versions of the future he faced, all the moves on the chessboard and all the ways he could react. What result would each produce?

The exercise was enough to induce a migraine, and his gaze unconsciously drifted to the roundness of her belly. He re-conjured that simple moment when she had set his hand against her taut warmth and let him feel the small piece of his brother, alive and kicking. The most perfect, unsullied parts of his brother, free of vanity and venality.

As he tried to recall exactly how that strange moment had felt, the fingers of slumber reached out to draw him under. His grasp on clear thought slid away and, for the first time in years, he drifted into a heavy sleep without any trouble at all.

* * *

The Queen's disappointment was palpable. Her pained expression as she skimmed her gaze over Hannah went into Hannah like a knife. She forced a polite smile to remain on her face while the older woman said something in a plaintive tone to Akin.

"Please speak English, Ummi. Hannah is American."

To be fair, his mother looked about as wretchedly unhappy as Hannah felt. And after sleeping in her clothes and coming off the plane in them, Hannah looked like a crumpled ball of sandwich wrap.

Queen Gaitha's face was lined with deep grief, but there was no mistaking the wrinkle on her nose as anything but an expression of dismay. She waved at a servant to show Hannah out.

Hannah refused to let anyone see how much the old woman's disdain affected her. She looked to Akin for guidance.

He nodded distantly to send her away, which stung, but he was about to be her husband in name only. She couldn't expect him to be some kind of savior who would make this easier. She would have to navigate it on her own.

A pretty young woman close to her own age introduced herself as Nura. She seemed kind and efficient and spoke several languages including English and Arabic. She explained that the wedding would take place as soon as Hannah and Akin had bathed and changed, then she would be able to rest until the baby came.

"Change into what?" Hannah asked with a semi-hysterical laugh. She didn't even have the overnight bag she'd left in her car when she had walked into the clinic.

"Oh, there are many choices." Nura drew her through a beautiful entry foyer that had an intricate mosaic floor and gold-framed mirrors on the walls. They reflected the round table in the center that held an enormous arrangement of fragrant flowers.

Hannah glimpsed a spacious waiting lounge with a view to a beautiful courtyard that had a free-form pool and abundant greenery casting shadows across the water. It looked like the Garden of Eden.

Nura brought her down a short hallway to

a salon of some kind. This must be the palace spa, Hannah deduced. It had a professional hairstyling chair with a huge mirror surrounded by lights. Scissors and brushes and styling tools were all at the ready. There was a manicure station and a pedicure massage chair like at a beauty parlor. On the other side of the room, there was a carpeted dais surrounded by full-length mirrors.

Nura slid aside a pair of doors and walked Hannah into a boutique. There was a selection of gowns in every color, shelves of shoes and handbags, scarves and belts and other accessories.

"I thought this one, but there are many beautiful choices." Nura produced a stunning caftan in silvery gray matte satin. It was demure, with long sleeves and a high neck, but beautifully embroidered with silver and gold beads. There was a matching veil that was so gracefully pretty that Hannah couldn't help exclaiming over it.

Since when was she such a *girl* who couldn't wait to try on a pretty dress for her forced marriage? Especially when she knew her figure left everything to be desired?

"Thank you," she said warmly to Nura, who was clearly pleased that Hannah approved of her taste. "If you could show me where I'll be staying, I'll bathe before I try it on."

"We're in your home, Princess."

"I don't think I made myself clear," Hannah said with a laugh of genuine amusement. "I know I'll live here in the palace, but I meant my bedroom. Is it close to this shop?"

"This isn't a shop, Princess. This is your dressing room. I am your personal attendant."

"I don't need an assistant," she said with confusion.

Nura looked at her with concern, as though she feared Hannah was spiking a fever. "Your assistant comes tomorrow, Princess. She will discuss with you your desires for the nursery and help you hire the nannies and the rest of your staff. I am your maid within these rooms, to help you dress and ensure your comfort—although your nurse will also stay in a room next to mine until you deliver, to ensure you and the baby remain in perfect health."

"But I don't need any of that!" Hannah blurted with real panic.

"You don't like me?" Nura's face fell in shocked hurt, as though Hannah had physically slapped her. "My mother attends the Queen. She has trained me my whole life to serve our future queen." She blinked wet eyes.

"Oh, Nura. I didn't mean to hurt your feelings." Hannah grasped her arm, realizing this might be her one chance to make a friend and she was blowing it. "This is all very new to me. I will very much need someone who understands how the palace works and what is expected of me. Of course, I like you and need you here to help me."

Nura gave her a trembling smile. "My mother likes to say a woman wears the spirit of the child she carries. If so, our future king will be very strong-minded and independent."

Hannah had thought she'd heard every old wives' tale possible, but that was a new one. She couldn't even laugh, though.

She dumbly followed Nura as she showed her into a palatial—ha-ha—bedroom. The *bed* was bigger than Hannah's old apartment. Massive windows looked onto the beautiful courtyard full of ornamental trees and vines and lushly blooming flowers. There was a fountain directly outside her bedroom window, creating a soothing sound and a screen of privacy should anyone be in the pool looking in.

Like who? she wondered with a half-crazed snort.

When she moved through the huge glass doors to take in the enormous space, she heard birdsong and saw several birds flitting about in a huge gilded cage.

Nura pointed out a door off the far end of the courtyard, barely visible behind its own bower of greenery. "Prince Akin's rooms. And this one leads there also."

She brought Hannah back inside and opened a slatted door from the bedroom into a private passageway.

Hannah felt as though the baby did a somersault. She grew warm at the proximity to Akin while also experiencing an urge to release a fully hysterical cackle. Might as well nail that shut, she wanted to say. He wasn't coming through it. Ever.

"The nursery is on the floor above. The elevator is near the kitchen."

Speechless, Hannah followed Nura into a ridiculous bathroom where the bath was a six-person jetted tub surrounded by marble columns. The shower was big enough to host a carwash. The extravagance of space was one thing, but the details! Gold faucets, hand-painted tiles, etched mirrors and silk rugs to drip her bubble bath froth upon. There was a velvet-covered bench in case she needed a rest between washing one hand and the other.

I can't do this was the uppermost thought in Hannah's mind as a muted bell sounded.

"The doorbell." Nura excused herself and hurried away.

"I have a *doorbell*?" Hannah muttered. She plopped down on the bench, head pounding. She couldn't even begin to process this, especially when her skin felt coated by travel, her mind still cottoned with jet lag.

She stripped down and turned on the shower, hoping it would clear the cobwebs.

The soap felt like silk and smelled of vanilla. The shampoo was a caress of tingling pineapple and rich coconut as it slid down her body. This would have been the most incredible shower of her life if Nura hadn't walked in and patiently waited with a bath sheet outside the cubicle.

"I'm not...used to having people see me naked," Hannah stridently told her, turning her back on the woman.

"Pregnant women are the most beautiful of all. Be proud that you carry a future king."

Clearly Nura's main duty was to bolster her mistress's fragile ego, and Hannah was feeling brittle enough to accept it. She let Nura dry and fuss and pamper her. When Nura rubbed moisturizer into her feet, she decided it was as good a reason as any to marry Akin.

Was she really marrying him?

Nura got her into a satin robe and slippers and they returned to the fancy dressing room. Nura pointed out the envelope that had been delivered. As Hannah sat in the chair to read it, feeling like a movie star refreshing her lines from a script, Nura began combing and drying her hair.

The document was their prenuptial agreement. When had Akin had time to prepare it? And how could he justify giving her half a mi— Wait. That was half a *billion* dollars for every year of marriage!

Hannah nearly fell out of the chair but kept reading. Along with granting her complete control over incidentals like decor in the nursery and whether her baby would be fed by bottle or breast, she was charged with the hiring and supervision of nannies and other infant caregivers. Provided she gave appropriate consideration to the teaching of Baaqi's language and customs, she had veto power on nearly every aspect of her son's early schooling. His later education would require a consultative process with the palace's best advisers, but her opinion would hold "profound weight" in those matters. There were stipulations for the baby's visitation with the Queen and time with Akin to learn how to rule, along with an expectation that her son make the palace his home. In all other ways, her son was regarded to be in Hannah's custody from birth until he was mature enough to make his own decisions.

The cordless phone rang and Nura stepped away to answer it, bringing it to Hannah.

"Will it suffice?" Akin asked.

Her heart gave a hard thump at hearing his voice. She looked at herself in the mirror, her reflection blurry because she wasn't wearing her glasses. She was prepared to agree. How could she refuse? But did he really want to attach himself to her? What did she bring to this marriage? Certainly not billions of dollars or international influence or even a sexy body that he could make use of via their shared secret passage.

"I don't understand," she said truthfully. "Are you really willing to give me this much power?" His mother had hated her on sight. Hadn't he noticed?

"Hannah." He had a way of saying her name as though he found her the most curious creature he'd ever come across and didn't know what to make of her. "You are the mother of our future king. All of those powers are yours regardless. I spelled them out because you asked me to."

"I'm…" She looked at the contract, but her thoughts were scattered. "I'm overwhelmed, Akin."

"Focus on the immediate. Sign it. Marry me. Then worry about the next task."

"I love how you act like our marriage is as simple an undertaking as registering to vote."

"It is. Polls close in one hour. I'll see you then."

One hour later, she was shown to a large hall where at least two hundred people were assembled. This was his idea of a small, private wedding?

She had felt self-conscious when she had realized he would see her like this. Nura had done her best, but lipstick didn't hide her braces. Heavy eyeliner only marginally helped her eyes look bigger behind her glasses. There was no way to look anything but near-popping pregnant, because that was what she was.

Akin looked incredible, of course. He wore a dark green robe with gold edging over a traditional white robe and headdress. His gaze skipped restlessly over her, showing no reaction, but her heart did a few twists and turns all the same, hoping he saw a little of something he might like.

At least the veil hid her butchered hair, but she still felt as though she was trying too hard. Like it was obvious she was trying to be pretty yet had nothing to work with.

Don't, she reminded herself. She'd spent too many years maligning herself, but she wished he was marrying her for some reason more than her baby. She wished he liked something about her. His dispassionate acceptance was almost worse than a stronger emotion like contempt or hatred.

The ceremony was conducted in Arabic. A young woman stood off to the side, quietly translating for Hannah. Parts of it seemed to follow his traditions, while others were more familiar to her as western customs. He didn't seem like a man who did things on a whim or out of sentiment, so she assumed there was a message for the gathered guests in the merging of their cultures.

She was so busy trying to track all those things she didn't feel the weight of her marriage sink in until Akin slid a ring on her finger. The split band setting lined with diamonds held a massive, glittering stone in the middle.

Her hand trembled in his and her breath grew uneven. He squeezed lightly as though offering reassurance, then gave her a similar ring to thread onto his finger.

It surprised her he would wear a wedding ring, especially one that was a masculine match to hers. His was a more robust setting with fewer diamonds on the band but an equally giant stone that was more deeply set.

It was heavy, and pressing the ring into place on his finger made her eyes sting. She blinked and the false eyelashes she wore fluttered against the lenses of her glasses.

Moments later, they were pronounced husband and wife. He lifted her veil.

That was the most difficult moment of all, when she felt as though all her shields were removed. She was as vulnerable as she could possibly be. He looked on her before all these people and she knew herself completely inadequate in every single way. He had let her put a ring on his finger as though this meant something, but it meant nothing.

Yet, his grave expression told her this marriage meant everything. He had made vows, same as her. For one tiny second, she almost believed they had truly promised themselves to one another.

His gaze slipped over her expression, likely reading all her silly dreams and hopeless insecurities. Her attempts and failures. Her hard-won pride and every humiliation she had ever suffered.

He gently cupped her cheek and his thumb caressed once, twice. He loomed closer. He was so tall! Her belly nudged into him and he paused with surprise right before his mouth touched hers.

Then his lips were against hers and her mouth trembled. How did such a sweet gesture make her feel as though she clutched lightning with her bare hands? Scorching heat suffused her, and her eyelids fluttered closed over her damp eyes. He started to draw back and she drew in the barest breath of protest, not ready for their kiss to end.

He returned with another sweet graze of his mouth over hers, lovely and tender and brief. He drew back, expression still solemn, but with a curious light in the back of his eyes.

Perhaps it was simply the flash of the cameras as they began to burst around them.

He turned her to face the crowd and it was done.

Hannah rose in the night, as she did about a thousand times every night. This time she knew she wouldn't get back to sleep. Maybe it was jet lag, maybe it was the baby, maybe it was a mind that had decided it was time to sift through the last thirty-six hours or so.

She and her "husband"—how surreal to think she had one—hadn't stayed long at their wedding celebration. She'd been introduced to a sea of faces and had eaten a few bites of unfamiliar foods that would have intrigued her if she hadn't been so overwhelmed. She had felt like an oddity in a zoo and was relieved when they made their escape.

She was hungry now, though. She searched up a banana from the bowl in the lounge and wandered outside to the courtyard to eat it, not bothering to pull a robe over her filmy blue nightgown. It was gorgeous out here. The birds were quiet, the stars twinkling, the fountain glowing and the air soft and warm. She lowered herself onto a well-cushioned lounger in the shadows beneath a tree and wondered if she had done the right thing or made a horrific mistake.

Just as homesickness and doubts began to prickle at her, there was a quiet movement from across the pool, the sound of a door sliding open.

Akin appeared in a loosely tied bathrobe, a drink in his hand.

The way he eased into a lounger and exhaled made her think he hadn't slept yet. He sipped, set the drink aside and let his head fall back.

She should say something, let him know she was here, but there was something companionable in silently sharing the night. Marital bliss? She smiled to herself in the dark, relaxing as she gazed on him.

He slid his hand into the opening of his robe to give a lazy scratch and she bit her lips against an embarrassed giggle. Maybe she should yawn loudly and pretend to wake up, then act surprised to discover he had joined her out here. She would just wait until he'd stopped...

He seemed to be scratching a long time. Was he—

Oh, good grief. He was. He was caressing himself!

She *really* needed to let him know she was here, but she was too mortified to move. Her mouth went dry and her throat locked up. She closed her eyes, but that was worse, because it only made her aware of the most luridly sensual feelings that were awakening inside her. Her nipples tightened and a pulsing, reflective ache accosted her loins.

She hadn't done what he was doing in ages, not feeling the least bit sexy lately, but suddenly she desperately wanted to touch herself and she wanted to watch him touch himself as she did.

What kind of pervert was she? At the very least, she definitely ought to keep her eyes closed!

But she didn't. She opened them to see if he had noticed her. He hadn't. She couldn't *really* see what he was doing, but his legs had shifted open. His hand moved beneath the drape of his robe. Tension increased its grip on him, and his hand moved faster...

She heard him inhale. She was right there with him, taut with anticipation.

He stilled and time stopped. Then his breath left him in a shaken exhale. His bunched shoulders relaxed.

For a moment, all she could hear was her heartbeat in her own ears. It was so loud he ought to be able to hear it clear across the pool.

He sighed again. It sounded more like relief than pleasure. Then, in a perfunctory move, he swiped the edge of the robe across his stomach, rising to remove it in essentially the same motion, as though he was well practiced at staining his robe and leaving it on the lounger. Then he walked naked to the steps of the pool.

Hannah sat there in astonishment, hot with voyeuristic lust, especially as she caught an eyeful of him stark naked, like he was part of some kind of man-candy calendar. The pale blue glow off the fountain threw shadows onto his brown skin, delineating his muscled chest and sectioned abs and *wow*. Sculptors were never that generous when they recreated a body like his.

Of course, he was still thick with his recent arousal, but her inner muscles clenched in longing as she drank her fill of the sight of him. She was still reeling from watching him, still ashamed that she'd done so, but not nearly as regretful as she ought to be.

She felt a bizarre kinship toward him, too. The matter-of-fact way he'd done it, as though it was one more chore like brushing his teeth, struck her as very forlorn. Was he as lonely as she was?

The water climbed to his knees, the middle of his thickly muscled thighs, and cut across his narrow hips to his waist.

She hadn't moved, but he suddenly stiffened. His arms flexed and his fists closed as he snapped his head to look directly at her.

Oh, dear. She braced herself for the worst dressing down of her life, one she absolutely deserved.

"I forgot you had access to this courtyard." His aggressive tension dissipated. "Go to bed. You need your rest." He stretched his arms before him and dove under, beginning to swim laps with tuck turns as if he did this as often as he did the other.

She husked out a laugh of relief, but... What had just happened? Why wasn't he angry?

Baffled, she shifted on the lounger, curling her legs up so she was more on one hip, the side of her face tilted into a small pillow so she could watch him. She wasn't sure why she did. She was still aroused, still terminally embarrassed, but there was something soothing in watching his body slide through the water in that rhythmic way. A splash of a turn and the long pull of his arms again.

Maybe she just wanted to know she wasn't alone here after all?

After about fifteen minutes, he stopped near her and folded his arms on the ledge. Here it came. She braced herself.

"Can't sleep? Why not?"

She blinked. "Why can't you?"

"Too much to do."

Dare she ask if manhandling himself was on his to-do list? To think she'd only put braces and making a baby on hers.

"Exercise is a waste of time," she said in a weak attempt at humor.

"It helps me clear my mind and fall asleep."

She bet it did. Oh, she was dying over here, glad the dark hid her fiery cheeks, trying to think how to smooth things over and coming up dry.

"Do you need something?" he demanded in a clipped tone that she imagined had entire regiments standing up straight.

Clarity. Reassurance. "I'd settle for a cup of tea, but I don't want to wake Nura."

"Your maid? Wake her. That's what she's there for."

"It's not important," she protested, touching where the baby was elbowing for more room. "This is all very strange. You have to know that, Akin."

"You'll get used to it." Zero compassion there.

Oh, she was going to have to grab the bull by the horns, wasn't she? "You must be angry with me. You have a right to be."

A single beat of surprise, then, "Anger, like all emotions, is a waste of time."

She frowned. "Do you really believe that?"

"I've been in combat, Hannah." Here was the quiet tone that refused to pull punches. "Anger provokes foolish acts of bravery. Rational thought keeps you alive. As you wisely put it to me, pick your battles. I don't pick unnecessary ones."

She let her head settle back onto the pillow as she absorbed that.

"But in future, if you want to watch me touch myself, *ask*. You owe me one." He slipped under the water and began swimming laps again.

Was that a joke? She covered her mouth, able to feel how hot her face became at the thought of owing him a reciprocal performance, but she couldn't help laughing into her hand. He had made a *joke*.

CHAPTER FOUR

AKIN WAS TAKEN aback each time someone congratulated him on his recent marriage. It was pro forma, and he had far more pressing matters to deal with. Immediately after his brother's death, various factions had decided Baaqi was at a weak point. Skirmishes had broken out on several fronts. Akin was still quashing them, but as the world absorbed the news that the much-harder-assed brother would be taking control while a recognized heir was weeks away from coming into this world, a tentative stability was beginning to settle over his country.

The fact that Eijaz's blood would eventually rule stirred up old feuds, though. Those who had admired Eijaz as dynamic and modern were elated. Those who had seen him as profligate and careless wanted nothing to do with his surprise heir.

And even though Akin's interest in such things as gossip, social media and fashion was less than zero, he was forced to sit through a report on how the world was taking the announcement of his marriage to the woman who was bringing that baby into the world.

"'I can't believe Hannah the Hag bagged a prince,'" one of his mother's minions read aloud while the palace public relations team wore appalled expressions. A handful of his closest advisers frowned with concern. "'She must have paid someone or switched the samples herself,'" the reading continued. "'There's no other way she could get a man to knock her up.'"

"She is my *wife*," Akin said through clenched teeth. "Never repeat those things. Sue them for libel."

"We've been taking steps, Your Highness, but these sorts of posts have persisted for weeks. We can't continue to ignore them in hopes they'll go away."

"What do you suggest I do?"

"Speak to her about making a statement? She's been refusing—"

"You *told* her these things are being said about her?"

"She was aware. They're online."

"These attacks are aimed at *me*. They're an effort to undermine my global standing and authority over Baaqi. But you had the audacity to take that to *her* doorstep and told her to solve it? She didn't ask for this! What the hell is wrong with you?"

"The Queen—"

He stopped short of dismissing his mother in front of the staff. There were certain lines he refused to cross no matter how ill formed his mother's views were these days. He walked out on the meeting, though.

He hadn't actually seen his wife much. They had dined with his mother twice since their wedding. Both occasions had been painfully stilted affairs where his mother refused to speak English. He couldn't discount that she was outright forgetting how, so he hadn't made an issue of it. He'd also traveled more than once, but he had daily reports from Hannah's nurse. He understood her to be uncomfortable and tired, which was regarded as normal when she was three weeks from delivery.

She hadn't emerged in the night again to watch him swim. He had confined his self-help activities to his shower. He was still perplexed—and yes, titillated—by the fact she had watched him. He didn't want to be tantalized by her. He rarely indulged himself with sexual imaginings. The desire for orgasm was an annoying appetite, like hunger for food. Yes, his body needed it eventually, but he wouldn't actually die if he went without sex, so he shouldn't be experiencing a twitch between his thighs right now, picturing an unpregnant Hannah gripping him while he stroked her slippery folds. What would she do if—

He yanked a halt on those lascivious thoughts as he arrived at her door. He hit the bell in warning and walked in.

Her maid appeared, widened her eyes in startled recognition, then dropped her gaze deferentially as she hurried to lead him into a small parlor where Hannah was sitting, reading her tablet. She set it aside when he appeared.

"Hello." She looked pale. Her eyes were bruised with lack of sleep. She wasn't smiling, which he suddenly realized she had done every other time she had seen him.

He found himself at a loss, not certain how to approach what needed to be said when there was no way to avoid hurting her with it. He should have been working through it on his way here, not pandering to explicit fantasies.

"How are you feeling?" That seemed a safe start.

"Let's just say the air conditioning is saving lives right now." She wasn't meeting his gaze and he didn't think it had anything to do with their intimate encounter the night of their wedding. They'd spoken several times since then and she'd confined her reaction to a self-conscious blush. This was shame, but from a different source.

He sighed and paced, waving the maid from the room.

"I'm not particularly intuitive, Hannah. Not when it comes to emotions. Dwelling on what someone might be feeling in a given circumstance has never served me in any profound way. I tend to let them deal with things however they wish and focus on taking action." He turned back to her. "But there are times when I must recognize that a sacrifice has been made. I realize you are giving something to our country at great cost to yourself." He nodded toward the tablet she'd set aside.

"I knew it would be awful, I just didn't expect it to be *this* awful." The break in her voice hit his chest hard enough to crack his breastbone. He didn't know how it hit so dead center, but it did. He quickly shored up inner walls against what felt like a sneak attack.

"You shouldn't have been told what people are saying. People in my position are targets. It's nothing to do with you."

She snorted. "It's *everything* to do with me. It's *about* me."

"It's not. You're the catapult they're using to throw stones at me. Dismiss it. Never think of it again."

"Oh, okay. I didn't realize it was that easy." She looked to the window onto the courtyard. Her throat flexed as she swallowed.

He might not be intuitive, but he knew intense pain when he saw it.

"They are strangers, Hannah. Their opinion of you means less than nothing."

"They're not strangers! They're people I knew from high school and college. People I worked with. The ambassador of my own country, who shook my hand at our wedding, called my pregnancy an 'unfortunate twist of fate.' *Your* people hate me. One of your PR people asked if I could go on a *diet*. What kind of *idiot* doesn't know how pregnancy works? Your mother can't even stand to look at me. She knows I'm not good enough to carry your brother's baby. Don't even try to tell me that's not true," she warned hotly.

"My mother is not in the market for new friends," he said flatly. "Do not take her cold shoulder to heart. That way lies madness, trust me."

Her gaze flashed up from beneath her crinkled brow. Another shift occurred. He had the sense of having revealed too much and reminded himself he had stopped caring about his mother's indifference long ago.

However, it was one thing for his mother to hurt him, and quite another that she was hurting his wife.

"Fire anyone on the staff who speaks to you in a way you don't like," he said tersely.

"I'm not going to fire anyone! That's not my place. And I'm not like that. I don't *retaliate*. It spurs them to act even uglier next time."

"There won't *be* a next time."

"There is *always* a next time," she hurled back at him. "And it's not like I didn't expect it. I'm just having trouble shaking it off this time."

He let that sink in. "You've experienced something like this before?"

"For God's sake, Akin, open your eyes! Of course, I've experienced this before. My entire life has been one bully after another. Except this time, I can't run home to Grammy or change schools or reinvent myself in a new job. I'll have to live with this sort of thing the rest of my life and my baby will—"

She closed her eyes, mouth pinched. A single tear tracked down her cheek and she struck it away before he had absorbed that he'd seen it.

"I'm the kind of person people want to pick on. I've never understood why. I'm nice. I shower," she defended on a choke. "But I've always been Lice Girl and Horseface Hannah and That Frigid Librarian. Why?" she demanded, eyes glowing with a sheen of angry, agonizing tears. "Explain to me why. Then maybe I'll be able to stop whatever it is that I'm doing wrong. Is it because I'm not pretty?" she asked with a pang in her voice. "Is that all it is? Because I can't change that."

The fractured crack in his chest was turning into a chasm. He knew this pain. He knew rejection so intimately; he couldn't see small red cars and snap-together train tracks without reexperiencing it.

Why was Eijaz exalted for his misbehavior and Akin's efforts to excel ignored? Why was his brother, who made jokes and pitched tantrums, so much better than he was, when he minded his manners and did as he was told? Akin had been given reasons for it at different times, but none that he had understood. Ever.

"Ignore me," Hannah said through a mouth that trembled, swiping impatiently at her wet cheeks. "I haven't been sleeping and I'm hormonal as hell. I'm not usually so weak."

She wasn't weak. He was having trouble figuring out exactly what she was. She baffled him continuously and put such an ache in his chest he couldn't speak, but she was the furthest thing from weak.

"Normally when I get maudlin, I go write a grant or work through the stacks to be sure all the books have been shelved correctly," she said with a weary sniff. "Got a library that needs cataloging?"

Don't do that, he wanted to say of her deflection, even though it was very much his own coping strategy. He would far rather take action than suffer the emotions that were trying to take him over as they stood here.

"We do have a library," he said, clearing a thickness from his throat. "It is scrupulously organized, but it contains books in several languages. You might find something that interests you. I can show you if you like."

"You're a busy man. As I've been told

every time I've asked about you," she said with a faint smile that died on contact.

Remorse pinched him. She was lonely and struggling and he had had no idea.

"I've seen the library," she dismissed with another faint smile. "It's beautiful." She inched herself to the edge of the cushion. "But right now, I need the potty. *Again*."

He moved to catch beneath her elbows and helped her to her feet.

"This is why I'm exhausted." Her mouth trembled between wry amusement and fraying courage. "Making a baby is hard work. Remember this some future day when I'm under your skin and you want to walk me into the desert and leave me there."

He did something he couldn't recall doing outside of a sexual encounter. He slid his arms around her and embraced her. Her belly made it awkward. He felt the small jolt of surprise that went through her as she realized he was hugging her and not letting her escape it, but after a moment, she obeyed his light touch on the back of her head and let her brow come to rest on his chest.

"It will be okay, Hannah." He didn't know

if he was telling the truth, and his conscience twisted, because what if it wasn't?

"Every time I convince myself you're a grouch who is avoiding me because you hate that you had to marry me, you do something I couldn't possibly expect."

"I don't hate that we're married." He tucked his chin to look down at the top of her head. Her hair wasn't a plain mousy brown as he'd thought. There were glints of cinnamon and copper and sable.

When had he become a poet, picking out strands of color in a woman's hair?

"You barely talk to me," she mumbled in accusation. "I'm pregnant with the baby who will usurp what you thought would be yours. You have to resent us."

"Oh, Hannah." He found himself playing with one little tail of downy soft hair that curled up near the base of her skull. "I barely talk to anyone unless I'm issuing orders. As for coveting that crown... I am filled with pity for your son. My only hope is that together we'll be able to mold him into a person who is strong enough to bear up under the pressure without being warped by it."

His deepest worry was that this baby would turn out like Eijaz, and all his efforts to maintain Baaqi's independence would be thrown away on a playboy's impulse.

"I'm counting on you being a good mother," he told her, running a hand down her spine, massaging her lower back. "Because I have no idea how to be a good father."

She stiffened and jerked back in what he read as rejection, even though he'd only meant his touch as comfort.

Her face wore shock and panic and the most beleaguered look as she said, "My water broke."

Akin called the nurse, who had Hannah transferred to the medical wing. He went back to work. He wouldn't be any use to her. The closest he'd been to a birth had been a feral cat in the back of a tent when he'd set up a presence near a vulnerable village some years ago. He had called his medic to keep an eye on things and remove the animals to a better home when it was all over. It had taken several hours, so he knew to expect that much.

But when he woke to a lack of announcements and arrived to an office going about their day, he blurted, "Is there any news?"

A sea of blank faces stared at him and someone tried to turn on the television.

"On my *wife*." It rolled off the tongue, but he didn't understand why. He suspected it was a possessive thing. His country belonged to his ruler. Virtually nothing in his world was his alone. Even Hannah would have to be shared with his future king, but he still liked being able to call her *his*.

One of his assistants picked up a phone and soon relayed that things were progressing normally. "A transfer to hospital should not be necessary, but they are prepared to do so if need arises. Every precaution will be taken so our next king arrives safely."

All the gazes dropped to the screens in front of them, signaling Hannah was forgotten.

She was actually quite small. Had no one noticed that? She only stood as high as his armpit and she was all belly. His brother had been built like him, an ox of a man.

She is not disposable, he wanted to shout.

That rush of inexplicable rage was enough to have him trying reflexively to compress his emotions back into their tightly packed bottle, but it only took an inane question about a political matter to snap his temper again.

"Who told her to lose weight? Find out who it was and fire them," he bit out to his assistant and shoved to his feet. "Tell the American ambassador he should go home and get control of his news outlets. He's not welcome here until he has personally apologized to my wife for the insults they've printed." He jabbed his finger on the table in front of the man in charge of his calendar. "Tell my wife's secretary that, under no circumstance, is the American ambassador to speak to her, in person or over the phone. If he writes to her, return his letters."

"I'm sorry," his assistant stammered. "I don't understand. How will he apologize if—"

"He'll have to speak to me, won't he?" Akin said in his deadliest voice.

Every single person who heard him slunk his head into his shoulders. His assistant, a stalwart servant of more than a decade, swallowed loudly.

"As you command, Your Highness. I'll attend to it immediately."

Akin was already stalking away, barking at the nearest person that he would be in the palace surgery, where the royal medical staff treated the family for all but the most serious ailments.

When he arrived, he was halted from proceeding down the hall to the delivery room by the nurse who'd been with Hannah since her arrival from New York.

"She's pushing. It's going well. Fast, which can be distressing. There's not much chance for her to catch her breath between contractions, but she's coping."

"She's in pain?" Why did that slice into him like a broadsword?

"Yes," the young woman said gently, her smile calling him a dimwit. Of course, Hannah was in pain. It was *childbirth*.

He looked past her. "It sounds like a party."
Was that *punk rock*?

"It's her birthing playlist. The staff are enjoying it. But it will take some time," the nurse said. "I'll notify you myself the moment there's news."

The nurse hurried back down the hall and he stood there like a chunk of furniture. A thousand priorities danced through his head, but he found himself cocking an ear, trying to hear the lyrics on the next song and the next. There was a string of angry-sounding "Hey, hey, hey!" and something about a bad movie and another complaining of times like this.

He pinched the bridge of his nose. What the hell kind of woman had he tied himself to? He had been worried enough to lose his temper and she was in there laboring like the world's biggest badass.

An angry scream, the kind he'd only heard in the throes of battle, ripped through the air, stopping his heart. The music abruptly silenced.

He shot down the hall and burst into the

room, hand reaching for the gun he wasn't wearing.

She was naked on the bed, a sheet draped over her waist, and an inchworm of a newborn, bright red and mewling, was being settled on her bare chest.

The music had been switched to a gentle piano over waterfalls and dolphins. It was so surreal he could only stand there in shock.

"Your Highness," the doctor said in a scandalized scold, even though he was the one looking up Akin's wife's skirt! A nurse draped a towel across Hannah so only the top of her chest and the baby's head were visible.

Hannah gently cradled her shaking hand around the damp wet hair of the infant. Her cheeks were tracked with tears. Her hair stood every which way and stuck to her sweaty face. She was florid with exertion, but when she smiled her metal teeth at him, he felt it like a punch in the heart. He had never seen anything so beautiful in his life.

"Come see him," she invited in a voice that rasped.

He was drawn forward as though pulled by a spell.

"I was convinced the scans were wrong and he would actually be a girl. I always wanted a daughter, but look at him. He's everything I could ever want or need."

The bond between a mother and her daughter was special. Perhaps one day, Akin found himself thinking, he might give her that girl she secretly yearned for. It was a foolish, wayward thought when he was quite sure the last thing she wanted to think about was childbirth again. He brushed his whimsy aside, but he couldn't resist touching her, gently squeezing her shoulder and letting his hand linger to caress her soft, damp skin.

"Well done, Hannah. Well done."

CHAPTER FIVE

HANNAH HAD DELIVERED early and even though it had been the most intense experience of her life, she and her baby were pronounced well two days later and sent back to her wing.

She then had a brief appearance where she presented the baby to the King so her son could be officially recognized. She'd been photographed looking wan and squishy, but she was too caught up in being a new mother to care what people were saying about her.

Officially her son was named for his father with a string of references to his family, the King, and the fact he was considered a miracle. Privately, Hannah called him Qaswar, which meant "lion," because he roared so loudly when he was hungry.

He always settled the minute she took him, which made her feel like the most powerful person in the world, but he slept as hard as he cried, and with his army of devoted nannies to change and bathe him, Hannah was able to get her rest. He also had a standing appointment to visit the Queen for thirty minutes every day, which Hannah began filling with gentle yoga.

She hadn't realized what a wet rag she'd become in those final weeks of pregnancy until, two weeks postpartum, she began to feel like her old self. Her energy returned along with her determination to steer her own destiny.

Everything had gone off-script with the discovery of her baby's father. This wasn't Syracuse. Her son was a future king and she was married. Although, who could tell? She hadn't seen her husband since the day she'd presented her baby to his parents. That stung, but she refused to let it get her down. This was her life now.

This was her *only* life. Two years ago, she had decided not to wait around for a man to "make" her happy. Akin might have barged into her delivery room like some kind of frantic new father ready to lay down his life for hers, but that had been out of concern for his nephew. She refused to read into it.

In fact, this scorned yearning that kept dancing in her periphery was exactly why she had chosen to have a baby by herself! She didn't want to spend her life looking at herself through a man's eyes, thinking, *If only I could lose ten pounds...* Well, it was *forty* now, if she wanted to be catwalk class. She already knew the futility of molding herself to a man's tastes. She would wind up shoring up his ego at the expense of her own sense of self-worth. She had done that her graduate year, when she had learned not to mention her grades because they outshone those of the man she was dating.

Her job was to love her son and herself. This might not be the life she had imagined, but she would not only own it, she would rock it.

To that end, she went through the things that had arrived from her apartment. She kept a few special items that added a personal touch to her living quarters and gave the rest to Nura to use herself or disperse among the rest of the staff. Nura acted as though it was Christmas, but that was still a few days away.

In fact, when Hannah unearthed the tiny tree she'd used in her apartment, she set it on her coffee table. It was only a foot tall, but it was sparkly and delighted her.

For the first time in years, she had a loved one to shower with gifts. Not that Qaswar needed a single thing—including Christmas. Baaqi was a Muslim country and her son would be raised with that faith, but thanks to his father's modern attitudes, Baaqi was broadminded toward other religions. Hannah only observed Christmas as a tradition anyway, not for holy reasons, but this was her baby's first one. She wanted to celebrate it.

One detailed list to her assistant later, everything she needed arrived forthwith, but wrapping it all had to wait. She had an appointment.

Hannah was finally out of maternity clothes and tied on a pale blue wrap dress with a nursing bra beneath. *Wow*, she noted as she stood in front of the mirror. Between the padding in the bra and the swell of milk, she had a chest that could get her hired in a booty bar.

Meanwhile, not only had she delivered a small monster of nine pounds, her body had stopped retaining the Persian Gulf. Her breasts were the part of her that stuck out most, not her waistline. She *had* a waistline.

Welcome back, she greeted it with a twirl, tempted to put on a pair of heels and see what that did for her figure, but who wanted to walk in those torture devices?

She did indulge herself by opening her private safe and having a rummage through it.

To mark Qaswar's birth, the Queen had presented Hannah with an opulent necklace. Its platinum setting was lined with round and baguette diamonds. The front was a remarkable fall of three strings with nearly two dozen massive sparklers interspersed with smaller diamonds. It was meant to be passed along to Qaswar's wife on the birth of his first child, she understood that, but she was still in awe that she possessed such a thing.

She didn't know when she would wear something that ostentatious, but she tried on her wedding ring. It fit! Pleased, she took out the other necklace she'd received to mark her son's birth. It had arrived with less fanfare and, compared to the behemoth from the Queen, this pear-shaped aquamarine pendant surrounded in diamonds was positively modest, but she had fallen in love with it the moment she saw it. Maybe it was the note that had endeared it to her.

With my deepest respect, Akin.

Respect, not regard, she had noted.

Oh, hush, she chastised herself as she asked Nura to fasten the necklace.

She returned to the lounge, where Qaswar was in the buggy that the nannies used to bring him from the nursery. Two hovered nervously, one armed with a diaper bag. Nura was giving Hannah an "Are you sure?" look as she helped her into an abaya and arranged a scarf to lightly cover her head. Nura would stay behind, but Hannah's assistant was pressing a brave smile across her face as she shrugged into her own abaya.

Hannah ignored their misgivings and

said, "Hold the door, please." She thrust her chin into the air and sailed through it. Four men waited beyond the foyer doors of her apartment. Two accompanied her son to his grandmother's each day; two were her own bodyguards.

Everyone fell into step behind her.

Hannah was reasonably sure she knew where she was going. She'd come back this way in a wheelchair after her stint in the private room where she'd delivered. The halls had been lined with smiling staff the whole way, all of them quietly and tearfully waving as they caught a glimpse of their future ruler.

Today, Hannah earned startled looks as she strolled along, taking a moment here or there to study a sculpture or painting. This place was a museum, loaded with stunning pieces. The floor tiles were art in themselves.

Each time she paused, her gaggle of ducklings would shuffle to a stop and wait patiently, then fall into step behind her for another few feet until she stopped again.

When she reached the main gallery, she couldn't help standing amid the rays of sunlight shot with rainbows as it poured through the colored dome.

"Isn't this beautiful?" she said with delight.

An elevator pinged nearby and she glanced over to see Akin stride out with his own entourage. Despite her stern pep talks, her heart leaped at the sight of him.

It was deeply unfair that he was so effortlessly gorgeous. His beard was scrupulously trimmed, his white kaffiyeh falling casually to flutter against his broad shoulders and frame his sculpted face. He wore a black robe with gold trim and an air of impatience as the sight of her stopped him in his tracks.

Those eyes! Nearly everyone she met here had dark brown eyes, but Akin's were like polished ebony framed in long, thick lashes. On anyone else, they would be pretty, but he wielded his gaze like a weapon, cutting his glance down to her toes and back up, sweeping across the people around her, then clashing back into her blinking stare.

"What are you doing here?"

"Good morning." She refused to let her good mood falter in the face of what she sensed was intense disapproval. "I'm going to the dentist."

"The dentist will come to you." His stern gaze flicked to her assistant, who cleared her throat, then to her guards. She heard what he was asking. Had no one thought to tell her that? "And the baby has no teeth."

"Yes, I know that," she said breezily. "But we felt like a walk."

"Did we." Akin's gaze stubbornly pulled hers, seeming to steal her breath as he did.

"Yes." She refused to ask him if that was okay. *Stop apologizing for existing* was definitely part of her happy-life plan, but it took all her mettle to stand there and clench her molars against the old habit. "Would you like to see him? I'm sure you'll notice he's grown since you last saw him." Akin had said he didn't covet the crown, but his lack of interest in her and Qaswar suggested otherwise.

"Since yesterday?" he asked dryly. He moved to peer down at the boy.

"You saw him yesterday? When?" she demanded.

"When he was with my mother. I see him every day when he's with her."

"I didn't know that." She could hear the accusation in her tone and his brows lifted in a subtle warning.

"Did you need to?"

"Are you hiding it?"

"No."

"Do you hold him?"

"Why?"

"Why should you hold him?"

"Why do you want to know?"

Because she wanted to see that, didn't she?

His cheek ticked. "I'm needed elsewhere. We'll talk about this another time."

The word "this" was barely inflected, but it left a deeply ominous dread inside her.

He turned away and she told herself, *Don't say it*, but it came out anyway.

"Have a nice day at work, dear!"

His shoulder blades flexed as though her words had struck like a stone between them. He walked away.

* * *

Akin had spent too many years cleaning up after his brother's impulses to be charmed by capriciousness on anyone's part.

After the day of Qaswar's birth, when he'd suffered a roller coaster of uncertainty as he awaited the birth, and then had his heart briefly ripped from his chest when he feared the unthinkable had happened, he had been forcing his world back onto an even keel.

It had only taken the act of stepping out of an elevator and finding Hannah strolling the palace like it was Central Park to feel as though the rug had been pulled out from under him again. He couldn't countenance it.

He wouldn't dress her down in public, but he intended to impress on her that he expected her to make his job of raising a competent king easier, not harder. He couldn't concentrate on human rights legislation when half his mind was taken up by wondering where she would take the baby next.

He stalked the shortest distance between their living quarters, the passageway between their bedrooms. Something about using it made it a clandestine act. He didn't know why. Her rooms had been set aside for his wife when he had arrived at adulthood and was given this wing. Hannah was his wife. There was nothing sexual about walking over to speak to her.

Except, despite his best efforts, he continued to have sexual thoughts about her. He blamed her doctor. In those moments after he had seen his nephew for the first time, Akin's mind had been stacked with thoughts of what needed to be done, like informing his parents and ordering public announcements. He'd still been reeling from the heartpunch of seeing Hannah holding that tiny baby. He'd been vaguely annoyed with himself that he hadn't been with her the whole time.

The doctor had drawn him aside and said something about realizing Akin was newly married and under many pressures, but Hannah couldn't meet the expectations of her new role until she had recovered.

It had taken a moment for the doctor's meaning to penetrate. When it hit, Akin had brushed the whole thing aside. He had told

Hannah their marriage would be platonic, and he had meant it.

At the time.

Then she had watched him on the night of their marriage, and he'd been fighting to concentrate ever since. He regularly imagined coming outside to find her naked in the pool. The fantasy always ended with him seducing her among the ferns and orchids.

It was annoying to be so distracted, and then, bam! There she was, right in front of him, dressed modestly like one of his countrywomen, but where the *hell* had her breasts come from? Mail order? They were spectacular. It had taken everything in him not to stare like an adolescent encountering his first underwear ad.

His loins twitched in remembrance. He should have showered before he came here, but no sense turning away now. He was at her door.

There was no bell. This passage was for their use only. The doors on either end were only decorative privacy screens of vented slats that allowed airflow and light into the windowless space.

He started to rap his knuckle, but that felt foolish. She was his *wife*. He might be second in line for the throne, but he was the height of authority in this wing.

He walked in and startled the maid who was plumping a pillow on the bed.

She squeaked with surprise and bobbed a quick bow, nervously directing him to the dining room, where he could hear Elvis Presley crooning about a blue Christmas.

When he arrived, he found Hannah swaying her hips, the scarf and dark abaya gone. Her short hair was smoothed to the side and clipped with pins decorated with ceramic roses. She wore a blue dress that turned her skin the color of cream. It was long-sleeved and belted closed, leaving a generous view of her chest above the crossed-over edges that formed the neckline. The fabric was a light knit that hugged her voluptuous figure adoringly.

Lust punched him in the groin. His wife was actually very*, tremendously,* hot.

She dropped her voice to croon a low "But *I'll*— Oh, hello." She jolted with surprise, then blushed and laughed at herself. "You caught me playing Santa."

There were a dozen gift boxes on the table. She was using ribbons to secure the lids and attaching name tags. Off to the side were cartons of unwrapped boxes of chocolates, books and colorful scarves.

"Are you sending things back to New York?"

"They're for my staff. And Qaswar's. He has thirty people dedicated to his care! I make thirty-one." She chuckled. "I'm counting the team who delivered him, of course. And I added my dentist to our list today. He said I could have my braces off early if I promise to be diligent with my retainer."

"We don't celebrate Christmas."

"I know. These are just tokens of appreciation that I'm choosing to distribute on the twenty-fifth of December. I've invited people to stop by for coffee and cookies if their time allows. Would you like to spend the day with us?"

"Us?"

"Qaswar and me." She leaned over the

table, gathering bits of ribbon and scraps of paper.

The pendant he'd given her fell forward, drawing his gaze to those magnificent breasts. He indulged himself with an un-adulterated eyeful, mouth going dry.

She glanced up and he realized she was waiting for an answer to a question he had forgotten.

She self-consciously straightened and adjusted the pendant. "I don't think I've thanked you in person for this. It's lovely and completely unnecessary, but thank you."

The color of the stone had reminded him of the oasis, the one place he was able to com-pletely relax. He hadn't visited in nearly two years and usually went alone. For some rea-son, he had imagined sharing it with Han-nah when he'd picked that out.

He didn't tell her that, only dismissing her words with "It was nothing."

The sweet light in her eyes dimmed and she dropped her touch from the pendant.

"Well, it's nice to be thought of," she mur-mured and gathered a stack of gifts with determination. She brought them to him. "Will you carry these for me, please?"

She picked up another stack and led him into the lounge. She set her lot on the coffee table and began fussing with them.

He left the ones he'd brought where she could reach them and moved to take in the framed black-and-white photos of New York that hung on the walls. There were a couple of photos of her as a child with an older woman—her grandmother, he presumed—and a terrible painting of a tropical waterfall. It had an HM signature, so he imagined it was something she'd painted herself. There was a colorful throw over the back of the sofa and an antique lamp with an elephant base and bronze fringe on the shade that was an absolute eyesore.

"This wasn't here when you moved in." It couldn't have been.

"It was Grammy's. When I look at it, I see her reading next to it."

A book with a bare-chested man sat beneath the lamp, a tasseled bookmark sticking out of it.

"Is this her book? I would have thought a

librarian would read something more literary or academic."

"Everyone thinks that. *I* thought it. For years, I made myself read the most depressing tomes out of peer pressure. It was like eating overcooked brussels sprouts because I'd been told they would put hair on my chest."

"Do you want hair on your chest?"

"No. Which is exactly what I'm saying. It was a dumb thing to do, so I put 'Read what I want to read' on my happiness list and you know what? I'm happier. Go figure."

"You have a happiness list?" She was piling up bemusement in him the way she was stacking wrapped gifts on the table.

"It's a work in progress. 'Try a new hairstyle' didn't land where I'd hoped." She pointed at the little pins crisscrossed to keep wisps off her face. "But I'm happy I *tried*. In that way it's a win. I also decided to only wear clothes that are comfortable, then I got pregnant and nothing felt comfortable, but I'm coming back to making that happen. I wanted a baby and got one. That has also deviated from plan." She sent him a look over her glasses that could only be called a "librarian scold," but it was such a good-natured one he rather liked it on her.

She moved a miniature Christmas tree to the top of her column of gifts.

"That looks ridiculous."

"I know. Isn't it great? And look." She showed him an envelope while making an O of her mouth. "What does that say?"

"Did you write that?" He took it and looked at his name neatly executed in Arabic.

"How's my penmanship?" She wrinkled her nose.

"I'm impressed." And confounded yet again. "You're learning Arabic?"

"Nura is an excellent tutor. My maid," she said at his blank look. "We're starting with the basics. Colors, clothing, food. Printing the alphabet."

He glanced at the name labels on the gifts, all written in her tidy hand. He knew the names of his key staff and approved raises and bonuses yearly, but he would never go to this sort of trouble.

He absently started to open the envelope,

but she gasped in mock outrage and held out a hand to take it back.

"I don't think so. If you want to know what this is, you can come back in two days."

"I can't take an entire day off and spend it with you, Hannah." It was absolute fact, but he felt like a jerk when her cheeky smiled dimmed.

"It's not a holiday you observe. I understand," she said, covering up her disappointment. "But if you can spare a few minutes to drop by, I hope you will."

So naive. "I don't take any days off," he clarified. "Even on the holidays we observe."

"Why not? Tell me a little about what you do all day." She waved invitingly toward the windows that looked onto the courtyard where her maid was setting a table.

What didn't he do? He followed her outside, thinking it was odd to see the pool from this angle along with his own lounge through the screen of greenery. It didn't bother him that she could see into his apartment. He was rarely there to do anything but sleep.

He sat and they served themselves from the tray of flatbread and dip, dates and cherry tomatoes. Hannah poured two cordials and tipped sparkling water into them.

"Is the supervision of the military still under your purview?"

"Completely. I meet with my commanding officers and advisers first thing every morning." And read their reports well into the night. The country's security required his constant attention. "I meet with members of parliament daily, as well."

"I've been reading about Baaqi's history. Your brother's decision to move Baaqi to a democratic parliament sounds as though it happened very quickly."

"Dreams happen overnight," he said flatly. "One can't expect to wake up and find they have become reality, though. It's been two years, but our neighbors, even some of our citizens, find the idea too western. My brother was trying to appease those who conspire to abolish the monarchy, but history is loaded with horrific examples of what happens when there is a power vacuum. The worst of society's evil moves in to seize it. My armed forces are kept busy ensuring our transition remains as civil as possible."

She sobered. "Should I be concerned about our safety?"

"I stay vigilant so no one else has to be," he said dryly.

She remained somber. "That's a lot on you."

"I'm used to it." He lifted a shoulder, finding her acknowledgment unusual enough to be uncomfortable. "There's no one else to do it when our government is still so new. My intention is that we'll continue to transition peacefully to a broader share of power, one that Qaswar can rule without the threat of constant uprisings. It's a delicate balance. When you saw me this morning, I was on my way into a trade negotiation. Those take time and they're draining, but diversification is necessary so we won't be dependent on oil resources forever."

"And the King? Given his health challenges, I imagine some of his responsibilities fall to you?"

All of them. He bit back a sigh.

"My father finalizes newly passed laws, but he doesn't have the stamina for reading long briefs. I review and approve them before he signs them off. He and my mother have ceased all of their ceremonial appearances, so I cut ribbons and visit hospitals. There is no end to petitions for our attention to smaller, more personal matters that we have historically settled. Today I learned of a Baaqi student who has gone missing in Australia. It's likely a hiking accident, not foul play, but a telephone call and a release of some funds go a long way to resolving things like that. I do as much as I can."

She closed her lips in thought. "That makes me sad. I mean, of course you should serve your country—you're above reproach for all you do, but I had hoped you would have time for being a father to Qaswar. Was your father this busy? What sort of time did he spend with you and Eijaz?"

Akin silently scooped dip onto a triangle of bread and ate it, considering whether there was any value in telling her how it had been. He rarely let himself dwell on it, but it had shaped him into the abrupt, uncommunicative man he was today.

That shell he'd adopted was as much a repellent as a defense, though. Since Eijaz's death, he had wondered if he and his father might find some approximation of the camaraderie or regard Eijaz had shared with the old man, but Akin was so used to not allowing himself to want it that he refused to let down his guard and make it happen.

Nevertheless, "I do want to be a father to Qaswar," he stated, even as he wondered if he had the capacity, given the fathering he'd had. "Eijaz had nearly thirty years to prepare for a role he was ultimately unable to fulfill. Qaswar will begin assuming formal duties as a child. He will rule at eighteen, sooner if he shows himself capable and willing."

"I was barely ready to look after myself at twenty-five. You really expect him to rule a country when he ought to be at college? I have very strong opinions about education, Akin."

"I'm sure you do, but you have to stop thinking of him as one of your middle-class American children." They had arrived at his purpose in coming here. "Qaswar is a prince, Hannah. And you are not a housewife who can throw Christmas parties for your staff and walk out with *our future ruler* as if you're part of some 1950s' television sitcom. We have protocols. Rules. I expect you to abide by them."

One spoiled, unpredictable future king was enough for his lifetime. He wouldn't raise another.

She sat straighter. "See, I knew you were annoyed with me, but how was I to know how you would react? This is the first conversation we've had in weeks."

That annoyed him. He was stretched so thin he ought to be in half a dozen other places right now, but he was here taking flak from her because he hadn't been dancing attendance like a newlywed?

"What did your staff say?" he challenged.

She hesitated before conceding, "That the dentist could come to me. But I was feeling cooped up. It's not as if I took him out of the palace."

"There was no need to take him out of these rooms."

"Is this my cage? Am I one of these birds?" She flicked a hand toward one of the cages. "Because I didn't see 'prisoner' in the fine print of our agreement."

"You're overreacting. I only want to be informed. We might have had guests."

"And you don't want anyone to see your hideous wife?"

"Don't be ridiculous."

"Oh, excuse me. Your *ridiculous* wife," she shot back. "I have spent my whole life trying to justify my right to exist. Do you even realize how many allowances and compromises I've already made to come here? How homesick I am?"

"For what? Syracuse?" he snapped. "Because you didn't make it sound as though you were that happy in America."

She sucked in an injured breath and sat straighter. "I was *trying* to be happy. I had a *plan*."

"You had a list."

"Don't disparage me for trying to achieve goals. I left everything that is familiar to me, and my *goal* is to make *this* feel like home," she spelled out. "So I went for a walk with my son. I could have left him behind, but I feel sick every time he's out of my sight. And you're taking me to task for that? You need to back off."

"I can't!" He slammed his hand onto the table, making her jump.

And now she'd goaded him into reacting and he was angry with himself. He rose abruptly, making his chair scrape, and strode several paces around the edge of the pool.

"I just told you what I'm up against, Hannah. This—" He circled his hand to encompass the paradisiacal courtyard that was his only refuge and only when he stole an hour late at night. "This is not real life. I give this to you and everyone else by keeping a firm grip on everything that happens in Baaqi. Don't fight me on that. For Qaswar's sake, you and I cannot be in conflict."

"I didn't ask to go to an all-inclusive resort for the rest of my life!" She stood, too, gesturing wildly.

"Neither did I," he bit out. "Yet here we are. And we can be enemies, or we can be allies. I make a particularly unpleasant enemy. Ask the ones I have."

"I can stand having enemies." She stalked toward him. "If you don't like me, that's your choice. What I won't do is allow an enemy to bully me and change my behavior. I won't buckle to your dictates and beg for your approval."

"Do you understand…" Warning rang from deep in his chest as he stepped close enough to bracket her toes with his own. "How much power I have over you?"

"Yes." She swallowed but met his gaze. Her lashes were quivering, her mousy brown eyes bright with fear behind her glasses, but she held his stare and crinkled her chin in determination. "You can threaten me and hurt me. Kill me, even. You can lie to my son and say I died or didn't want him. You hold all the cards, Akin." Her voice shook with intimidation that turned to resolve. "But I can never raise a son strong enough to face all he faces if I can't stand up to the man who will have the most influence over his life."

This woman. She had to know she was playing with fire. He wanted to crush her, he really did.

But there was something so glorious about the way she held his gaze and held her ground when her hands were in anxious fists and he could see her pulse racing in her throat. It wasn't just her son she was standing up for. It was for herself.

That conviction of hers struck a match in him that was the furthest thing from anger. It was hot and passionate and possessive. It was a fire so bright it could destroy him, yet he wanted to throw himself into it.

"This is who I am." Her voice shook. "I refuse to backslide into waiting around, hoping my life will drift in a certain direction. I'm going to go after what I want. Do whatever you have to in response to that, but this is who I am."

He did. He gave in to the compulsion to set his hands on either side of her head and tilted her mouth up to his as he swooped down, remembering at the last second not to rake her lips against her braces as he fit his mouth to hers.

She gasped and stiffened, hands flying up to take hold of his arms.

He braced himself for a scream, for an attempt to shove him into the pool. He would have released her, he wanted to believe he would have, but she only dug her nails into the tender skin on the inside of his wrists and stood very still, mouth trembling against his own.

He had never touched a woman in anger and that was not what this was, although there was anger in him as he took ravenous possession of her mouth. Sexual frustration had its talons in him along with a deep, indignant fury that he was being overthrown in a way he couldn't combat—because he didn't know how to fight her. He didn't want to fight. That was the issue. These lips said the most outrageous things and he wanted them to *do* outrageous things. He wanted them everywhere on him. Whispering against his ear and biting his neck and closing around his stiffening sex.

He wanted *her*.

He couldn't deny it any longer. He absorbed that undeniable fact as he roamed his mouth across hers, learning her edges and corners and softness and taste, coaxing her to kiss him back with a soft cling of her lips to his own. It became the tenderest act of punishment he had ever delivered. He was the one being punished. He understood that at a hidden level as a wildfire he couldn't douse swept through him, burning past any good sense that remained, urging him to beg for her to *meet his expectations.*

A baby's cry reached them, and Hannah gave a fresh gasp as she jerked her head back, staring at him in abject shock.

CHAPTER SIX

AKIN LET HIS hands fall to his sides while she turned and hurried inside. Shame hit him in another lash of punishment. They couldn't be enemies, if only for his nephew's sake, but he'd taken the first steps of aggression himself. How would she retaliate?

Akin watched her through the glass. Her voice carried in a muted, flustered sound. Her body language was tense, but her entire demeanor changed as she gathered the baby and crooned to him, nuzzling his cheek.

Firstborn, Akin thought enviously, punched in the gut so hard he had to look away. Another proverbial welt rose as he realized he could never give her another baby. He couldn't put his own child through the agony of being the unchosen one.

I feel sick each time he's out of my sight. The Queen still felt that way about Eijaz but had never once behaved as if she wanted Akin anywhere near her.

He hadn't realized his gaze had fallen into the middle of the pool until a noise drew his attention back to the table where Hannah was retaking her seat. She'd draped a light blanket over her shoulder. Qaswar fussed with growing ire.

"I know, I know. I'm hurrying," she assured the baby. "Poor starving thing. You'd think you were abandoned on a doorstep. If this king thing doesn't work out, you definitely have a career on Broadway."

"What are you doing?" Akin hadn't expected her to come back out, let alone—

"He's hungry. So am I." She fiddled beneath the blanket and adjusted the baby.

The frantic wails ceased. She sighed and took a long drink from her glass. "Nursing makes me thirsty, too."

Akin looked toward the pool entrance into his own quarters. "Should I leave you alone?"

"Does it make you uncomfortable to be here while he eats?"

Was that what he was? This wasn't a circumstance he'd ever encountered. He wasn't used to being drawn into private moments of any kind. It felt like an overstep, the same way it had when he discovered she read romance novels and had a happiness list.

"Can I say something before you go?" Her voice was tentative and not quite steady. Her lashes stayed down, hiding her eyes while her cheeks wore scorched flags of heightened emotion.

He folded his arms, certain she would berate him for kissing her. He ought to regret it, but it wasn't that simple. Not when she had responded with a sweet heat that had been as unexpected as it was exciting. He was still hard and wanted more. He wanted to delve the very depths of her passion and she was going to call him a brute and tell him to go to hell.

"I'm trying to make the best of this, but it's been a difficult adjustment. Motherhood is. You can't imagine any of this has been easy for me, Akin. But every time I hold my son, I'm reminded that I'm here because your brother helped me make him. Not intentionally, but the stars aligned, and now this is my life. You're right that I can't deny him his birthright. I want to prepare him as best I can, and I want him to be safe while he grows into it. I didn't mean to sound ungrateful for all that you do for his sake. I'm incredibly grateful for *him*."

She lifted earnest, damp eyes, saying nothing about their kiss.

He was arguably the most powerful man in this country and definitely on the top ten list in the world. He was revered and feared in military circles, known for his clever strategies and triumphs against grim odds.

Yet Hannah undermined him with a few words that weren't even flattery. They weren't about him directly, just sincere sentiments that took all the air out of him. He would be furious at this ability of hers if he wasn't so fascinated by how artlessly she wielded that particular weapon.

He sighed, pushed his hand through his hair.

"My brother was very unpredictable, Hannah. It's disloyal of me to criticize him, but his nature was very mercurial, and he was always given absolute freedom." Never held to account. Never forced to pick up pieces. That was Akin's job. "Thankfully, he was essentially good at heart. He wanted progress for Baaqi, but in a very idealistic way, not with a desire to do the hard work of it."

Akin pressed his lips flat, glancing toward the open doors and lowering his voice so only she would hear him.

"In many ways, he was motivated by the fact that ruling a country *is* work. With my father ailing, Eijaz was being called upon to do more. He thought he could delegate to a parliament and continue living however he liked. There was no sense of order when he declared we would hold a general election. No plan. He threw a rock into a nest of hornets and ran away to post photos of himself climbing glaciers in Antarctica. I had to deal with the fallout from all his whims. This has been a particularly challenging one." Akin sealed his lips against any further disparagement of a dead man.

"You're worried that I'm like him, doing things you can't predict."

"I know you're like that. You surprise me every time we interact." And much as he wanted to dislike her for it, he found it made her that much more appealing.

"I want to reflect well on my son, you know. And you." She said that with a deeply vulnerable look.

You don't want anyone to see your hideous wife.

Her self-esteem had been thoroughly trampled and he didn't know how to address that. He wouldn't have kissed her if he didn't find her desirable, but he was regretting that he'd lost control and broken his word. The one thing he'd always prided himself on was having more self-discipline and forethought than his brother. A sense of consequence to his actions.

"Will you eat with us so you and I can make our peace? I don't want us to be enemies."

Every time he thought he was being given more than he could handle with her, he just as quickly discovered there was an opposite side to the coin, one that put a completely different face on the situation. She was generous and forgiving, and he was drawn to that strange fire in her like a lost traveler in the desert on a cold night.

He retook his seat. He was hungry and the food was here. That was what he told himself. He was only being practical.

"Do you visit Qaswar when he's with your mother because you wouldn't have time to see her otherwise?"

He could have agreed and left it at that. Allowing people into the private spaces of his own life was as foreign as being granted admission to hers, but the situation with his mother was one of those excruciating realities where denial only made it worse.

"She needs a full-grown reminder that Qaswar is not Eijaz. In her mind, Eijaz has been reborn. Qaswar's presence brings her comfort, which I can't begrudge her, but she wants to believe he *is* Eijaz. She verges on taking credit for him." He feared if he wasn't strict about how much she saw the baby, she might try to claim him completely.

"Does she suffer dementia or some other condition?" Hannah asked with hushed anguish.

He nodded. "That's confidential. Not many

know, and her grief has made it worse. The reality of Eijaz being gone is beyond what she can accept, not when a beautiful replica of him allows her a more comfortable delusion. It's not healthy for either of them, but I don't have the heart to force the truth on her. Her pain is real. Her mental state is irreparable. There are no solutions."

"That's tragic. You must be awfully worried for both of your parents. I'm so sorry." Her hand came out to clasp his wrist.

He looked at her narrow hand, so pale and delicate, smooth and warm. He was baffled by it. Perplexed by her words and tone. Comfort? *For him?*

She withdrew self-consciously. "My grandmother had arthritis and some heart trouble, but her mind was always sharp. I can't imagine how difficult it must be for you."

A strange sensation ballooned in the base of his throat. He swallowed it away before it could take hold.

"We do what we have to." This was why platitudes existed—to be used to gloss over otherwise intolerable moments.

"Would it be helpful if I visited with your mother when Qaswar goes? I had the sense she dislikes me, but I understand now."

"I can manage," he assured her.

"But you don't have to," she said gently. "I wish I was reading above a preschool level in Arabic. I can't offer to help you with your law reviews, even though I have a reputation for being both a miracle worker and a complete pest when it comes to thorough research."

"I have no doubt." He smeared up the last lick of dip with a corner of flatbread.

"You've seen my work with ribbons. Feel free to put me to work on cutting some."

"None of this is necessary, Hannah."

Her good humor faded to a crestfallen hurt that she tried to disguise by looking toward his side of the courtyard.

"Are you trying to let me down gently? We promised each other honesty, Akin. If I'm not presentable enough to reflect well on the palace, please say so."

Your hideous wife.

It galled him that anyone had ever said a harsh word against her. *Stay here*, he wanted to command, so he would know unequivocally that no one could touch her.

"I'm not used to accepting help. It hasn't been an option. When we married, I thought it was purely for his sake." He averted his eyes as she started to withdraw the baby from beneath the blanket. "My mother gave up her duties sometime ago, so it didn't occur to me that you could, or would want to, take on any of them."

"I would be honored to do anything you need." She handed the baby across. When he stared blankly, she added, "Can you hold him please?"

Akin hadn't wanted to admit this morning that he hadn't actually held his nephew. He'd observed how the boy needed his neck supported and was handled like a sculpture made of spun sugar. Akin didn't want to be the one who broke pieces off him.

But here the infant was filling his hands, light yet sturdy, fighting fists clenched, naked brows scrunched as he blinking crossly beneath his cap of wispy black hair.

Akin couldn't help the twitch of empathy

that quirked his mouth. "Nothing good ever lasts, does it?"

"Nothing bad does, either." Hannah finished her wardrobe adjustment. "I've always needed to believe that, anyway," she said as she snapped the blanket away and draped it over Akin's shoulder. She then guided him to bring the boy up to rest against it. "So he doesn't spit up on you. Rub his back until he burps."

A nanny was hovering on the other side of the glass, ready to step in. Akin had far more important claims on his time than coaxing gas, but he kept the little body cradled to the hollow of his shoulder, one thumb making passes across the boy's tiny back.

The scope of responsibility Akin carried on this boy's behalf often threatened to break him, but for one moment, Akin was drawn into the bubble of safety and contentment he created for everyone else. Relief sank through him.

Hannah sighed. "I wanted to see that." Her expression was so full of sweet enchantment that Akin nearly lost a tooth.

Holding the boy became an indulgence. A

weakness. He shouldn't be gaining anything from the baby, only giving. Akin glanced and the nanny rushed out to whisk the boy away.

Hannah's expression turned doleful. "You don't want to be friends with me, do you?"

"I said 'allies,'" he reminded.

"That's all?" She searched his expression, her own gaze confused.

It was the moment to address the kiss. The moment to admit he would like a more conventional marriage that included the sharing of his bed, but sex meant children, and "friends" was far safer.

"You may have Christmas," he decided abruptly. He wasn't a monster. "And I will give thought to the formal duties you might take on for the palace. If observing tradition is your thing, perhaps you'd like to supervise the ceremony that will mark my father's formal retirement, where I will be appointed Regent in his place."

"Really?" Her smile burst like sunshine. "I would love that! I organize the dickens out of a cap-and-gown ceremony. You won't be disappointed. As for other duties, I would be happy with anything to do with literacy or education, particularly for girls. Women's health or childhood immunization or—"

He held up a hand. "There's a saying about idle hands that applies double to you, doesn't it? If I don't keep you busy, you'll plan a wet T-shirt contest before I can stop you."

"I'm holding one during the Christmas party. I'm pretty sure I'm going to win."

He closed his eyes, refusing to laugh. "Talk like that does not make your case as a suitable representative of the palace."

"But it's on my happiness list."

"Winning a wet T-shirt contest?" He was so tempted to pick her up and throw her in the pool.

"No, but I should add it, shouldn't I?" Wicked laughter was dancing behind the lenses of her glasses. "No, saying funny things is on my list. If I think it, I have to say it and not worry how people will react. Most people like funny people, though, so the odds are good it'll be a win-win."

"The day your bra size is announced in the headlines is the day I seal the doors on this apartment myself."

"See? I like you when *you* joke. It makes you seem almost human."

"I'm not joking." He rose.

"Where are you going?" The way she tilted her chin up made him want to cup it and kiss those lips again.

"I have been idle long enough."

"But that was only the appetizer."

Exactly. And like holding the baby, bantering with her was beginning to feel like an amuse-bouche before a grander meal. Like there was more to come. Courses to be savored that would be infinitely satisfying. "My people will be in touch to discuss the ceremony."

He walked around the pool to reach his own wing, mostly so he could spend those extra few seconds with the feel of her gaze on his back.

Hannah was lost in a cowboy catching a barrel-racer under some mistletoe when a tingling awareness had her absently glancing up.

Akin had appeared from seemingly thin air and stood watching her.

A jolt of electric surprise shot through her. She had been thinking nonstop about him and his unexpected kiss. How he'd cupped her cheeks as though sipping from a china bowl yet managed to shatter every thought in her head.

She'd been so shocked that she had hurriedly stammered right past it, using Qaswar as a shield, talking about anything *but* their kiss, but the memory hadn't left her. It rushed to the forefront of her mind now and caused an acute blush to sweep over her. She lowered her gaze.

The image of him stuck in her brain, though. He wore black trousers and a light gray tunic that closed with three snaps at his shoulder and half a dozen down the side. It was long-sleeved and plain, but it clung to the contours of his shoulders and upper chest, accentuating his physique.

"Where is your maid?" Akin moved to glance at Qaswar sleeping in his cradle.

"I gave everyone a few hours off."

His cheek ticked. "Because it's Christmas?" He eyeballed the pile beneath the tree that had been reduced to three small boxes.

The trays on the sideboard held mostly crumbs.

"The guards are still at the door. They have even more adherence to duty than you do. Help yourself."

He did, demolishing a square of shortbread in one bite, then used one hand to stack the remaining gingersnaps and dealt them into his mouth, one by one.

She plucked the envelope from where it sat in the branches of the tiny tree and rose, suddenly deeply self-conscious about the gift she'd prepared. It had seemed like a nice gesture at the time, but that had been before their strange blowup and makeup the other day.

Was their kiss part of the former or the latter? She still didn't know.

She cleared her throat and said, "Merry Christmas" as she offered the envelope.

He turned over his free hand. She hadn't realized he was holding anything, but it was a small box with a silver wrapping.

"You don't celebrate Christmas."

"In the interest of diplomacy, I reciprocate gift-giving when it seems appropriate."

"Ah. This must be a lapel pin of your flag, then?" She shyly accepted it.

"Crib notes on your Constitution?" he guessed as he took the envelope.

He had to know how disarming he was when he showed her those glimpses of humor beneath the intimidating mask. He probably did it specifically to disarm. The way he watched her might have been designed to make her aware of herself as a woman. She became hyperconscious of every small thing about herself, from how she stood to the fit of her bra to the faint tremble of nerves in her fingers as she began to peel the gift open.

She watched surreptitiously as he broke the seal on the envelope with a practiced flick of his finger and withdrew the pages. It would take him a moment to realize what it was, so she quickly finished unwrapping hers. It was a beautiful pair of earrings that matched her pendant.

"How did you know that getting my ears pierced was on my list?"

"I didn't realize they weren't." His gaze flicked to her earlobe and swirling eddies of tension invaded her belly. From a *look*. At her *ears*. How would she react if he ever genuinely ogled her?

"Well," she babbled self-consciously. "This gives me the motivation to get past my squeamishness. Thank you. They're beautiful."

"You're welcome," he said absently, face hardening as he returned his attention to the outline before him. "You're giving me a biography?"

It had seemed like such a nice idea. Now she felt like a rock god's most enamored and possibly annoying superfan.

"I mentioned that I've been reading up on your history," she reminded him. "Your mother has one, your father has four and your brother has nine—but only two of them are authorized. The palace refused to bring in the ones that weren't." Heaven help them all if Qaswar developed his father's streak of self-indulgence. "Everything on you is piecemeal articles in a dozen languages all over the place, even though…"

She didn't want to criticize her son's father or grandfather, but from what she'd read,

Baaqi's current state of tentative peace and growing prosperity was more Akin's accomplishment than the King's. Akin hadn't got a quarter of the credit he deserved.

"Well, it seemed as though it was a missing piece of a puzzle. The palace librarian said it was a matter of someone leading the charge and putting up funds. I have a ridiculously generous allowance, so I contacted the history department at your university. A professor agreed to select a group of students to make it happen. Are you pleased? Irked?"

He let his hand drop to his side. "I'm not looking for accolades, Hannah."

"That's not what it is! *I* want to know about your actions and accomplishments. Think of it as a record for Qaswar and his own children. You can't have a near twenty-year gap in Baaqi's history that just says, 'His uncle held the fort for a while.'"

His mouth twitched with dismay, but he conceded her point with a half nod. "I suppose if it's a factual account, you may continue. Do not paint me as any sort of hero. I've been doing my duty to my king and country. That's all."

"Of course." She opened her mouth to say more but closed it again.

His brows went up. "If you think it, you have to say it."

She bit her lips. "I only thought there was a joke there about your heroics in saving him from being the son of an academic librarian, but it didn't arrive fully formed."

"Don't disparage yourself." It wasn't a quip. He used the commanding tone that held such authority it seemed to land in the middle of her chest and expand, knocking apart all the old framework and leaving room for new views.

She folded her arms defensively as she realized she was still denigrating herself when she had promised herself she would stop. It was even more disturbing that he had noticed and refused to hear it.

"You see?" he said, voice pitched quieter but becoming more impactful. "I protect him against everyone, even from insults to his mother when she forgets that she deserves respect."

She could have cried. Really. She blinked hot eyes and admitted, "Sometimes it's eas-

ier to make a joke than feel all the feels."
She fought to keep a smile pinned onto her
mouth, but it slid sideways.

"Sometimes it's easier not to feel anything
at all," he said with a gravity that kept sinking deeper and deeper into her.

His gaze hovered on her mouth and she
thought he might be thinking about kissing
her again, but his attention flicked away. His
eyes lingered on the baby before moving to
the door.

"I've asked the chef to roast a chicken for
dinner if you'd like to stay and eat with me?"
she offered.

"The helicopter is waiting."

Her heart pretty much dropped off a cliff.
"I didn't realize you were leaving. Will you
be gone long?"

"Two weeks."

An eternity.

"Will you go with Qaswar to visit my
mother?" he asked.

That took her aback, but she nodded. "If
you want me to, of course."

"Thank you." He started to turn away,

looked at the paper in his hand and came back. His hand cupped her cheek.

She lifted a hand to his chest as his mouth came close. He paused. "There are more things we should talk about. I don't have time right now."

"Does it have to do with the fact we're people who kiss now?"

"It does." He waited another beat, as though giving her a chance to argue that development.

She only looked at his smooth lips and watched his head dip, willing her heart not to race so hard it ran itself into the ground. Her eyes fluttered closed as she savored the way he took her mouth captive. Her fingers unconsciously closed in the fabric of his tunic while her lips flowered in offering.

His arms went around her, and she melted into him. He was so tall and strong, holding her nearly off her toes as he gathered her into his chest and crushed her tight, his hunger making her feel infinitely desirable as he consumed her.

Far too soon, he set her back and steadied her. She was utterly befuddled, panting and blinking eyelids that felt too heavy to keep open.

He nodded as if that was the reaction he'd been looking for and left without another word.

CHAPTER SEVEN

KNOWING THE QUEEN suffered cognitively allowed Hannah to let the older woman's vague hostility roll off her back. If Queen Gaitha didn't want to speak English or acknowledge her at all, that was fine. There was nothing wrong with the older woman's maternal instincts. She might call Qaswar by his father's name, but she held him with incredible tenderness and murmured lovingly to him the entire time.

Nura's mother, Tadita, was Her Majesty's personal attendant. She hovered attentively, agreeing with the Queen if she happened to say something. Her tone was always soothing, as though she was actively working to keep the older woman's mood calm. The Queen grew despondent when it was time to give up Qaswar to the nannies but otherwise

seemed in good spirits. She always bright-
ened when they arrived again the next day.

All went well until about the fifth day. The
Queen had just given up the baby to Tadita,
who gently placed him in the buggy. Hannah
always brought the baby into Queen Gaitha's
private parlor herself, leaving the nanny and
bodyguards outside the room.

The Queen frowned at her as she rose to
take him out. "Why is the nanny dressed
like that?" she asked Tadita.

"This is Prince Akin's wife, Your Majesty. Remember? Princess Hannah." Tadita's
smile at Hannah begged for understanding.
"She is Qaswar's mother."

"Who is Qaswar?" The Queen frowned in
confusion, looking between Hannah and the
buggy. "And she is married to Akin? No. I
hate Akin. I love Eijaz. Why is she taking
him?"

Tadita glanced helplessly at Hannah, mortified by her mistress's words.

"Qaswar is Eijaz's son, Your Majesty,"
Hannah said in the most gentle and reassuring tone she could muster. "Akin mar-

ried me so I could bring Eijaz's son to be here with you. He will rule one day, as your husband does."

"But where is Eijaz… Oh." The Queen remembered and her eyes filled with sorrow. "Akin should have been the one to die. I never wanted him. I loved Eijaz so much."

Hannah was appalled, but she didn't let it show on her face. She might even have dismissed the Queen's sentiment as the ramblings of dementia, but the guilty horror on Tadita's face left a lump of icy understanding sitting heavily in her belly.

Tadita was making noises of comfort as if she'd witnessed this kind of resentment many times.

Hannah slipped away, but she could hardly breathe. Little things clicked in her mind—the way Akin always seemed to be recognized as being ancillary to the rest of his family. Eijaz was clearly the favorite who had been allowed to do anything he liked, while Akin was the one to do the real work of running the country. She remembered what he had once said about his mother. *Do not take her cold shoulder to heart. That way lies madness, trust me.*

"Are you feeling unwell, Princess? May I get you something that appeals more?"

Nura's voice snapped Hannah out of her reverie to an awareness of birdsong and the tinkle of the pool fountain. She was eating her midday meal in the courtyard as was her habit, but she hadn't touched her lamb and rice.

"I'm thinking about my visit with the Queen today," Hannah admitted. "She said something that left me wondering."

"My mother feels very fortunate to see the young Prince each day when you visit Her Majesty. I tease my mother and say, 'Yes, but I see him much more.'" Nura topped up the water in the glass that Hannah had barely touched. It was the sort of banter they often enjoyed, but Hannah had the strangest feeling Nura was trying to distract her.

"Nura, I know you and your mother are very loyal. You would never gossip about me or the Queen, not even with each other."

"Never, Your Highness!" Nura seemed to

blanch beneath her light brown skin at the mere idea.

"But can you tell me, when you trained to become an attendant, did you work with your mother directly in Her Majesty's presence?"

"Oh, yes." Nura was shifting her weight, clearly wary of saying too much but wanting to impress on her how well qualified she was. "The Queen has retired from many of her duties, but when she was active, she required many hours of preparation and clothing changes. I assisted my mother as soon as I could fetch and mend. Later I arranged much of the incidental shopping. I cleaned shoes and jewelry and tended the Queen's birds in her courtyard. I was the lead maid of four who kept the royal chambers under my mother. Is there some particular task I've neglected that you need me to do? Please tell me."

Hannah started to say no, but turned it into, "I think there is some information you might be able to give me, something that will help me as I learn to make my home here. I need to know more about the Queen's regard for my husband."

If Hannah had ever seen someone confronted with the barrel of a gun, the expression on Nura's face was it. Hannah's niggling intuition turned into a heavier dread.

"I understand that Her Majesty has not been herself since losing Qaswar's father," Hannah said gently.

"No mother should have to face losing a child," Nura said with anxious sympathy. "And she lost a daughter many years ago. You may not know that."

"No, I didn't. That's tragic." It was. From the outside, Akin looked as though he had everything, but she was getting the sense he'd had very little of the things that counted. "It sounds as though she loved Prince Eijaz very much."

It sent her into agony, thinking of Akin risking his life for his country—for the very brother who had been favored over him. What if he had died in battle? Would his mother have mourned for him the way she did for Eijaz? She wanted to believe the Queen would have but had to wonder.

"Everyone thought very highly of the Crown Prince," Nura said, her voice barely above a whisper. She knew what was coming and so did Hannah.

"But how did the Queen feel about Prince Akin?" Hannah prompted, bracing herself.

"I—" Nura was wringing her hands, gaze casting about as if she were hoping a dropping piano would save her from continuing. "My mother once said that every mother loves her children, but some mothers love one child a little more."

"And some love certain children less?"

"Not through any fault in the child," Nura said hastily. She looked miserable as she gazed toward the aviary. "But I think that can happen sometimes, yes."

Hannah's heart grew thin as it stretched toward the doors to Akin's empty chambers and further afield to wherever he was. She drew a pained breath and nodded understanding.

"Thank you, Nura. When I visit the Queen, I see how much your mother cares for her. It must be a great comfort to Her Majesty to have someone she knows so well at her side when she is not feeling as well as she could. I know I'm very fortunate to have *you*.

Like you, I only want good things for Baaqi. Thank you for helping me understand the things that affect my son and my husband."

"Of course." Nura looked relieved to escape as Hannah let her take her plate. They didn't talk about it again.

Akin was exhausted. He took his scotch—a vice he'd picked up from a friend at Oxford—to his lounger beside the pool. His butler had taken to leaving a towel out here so Akin wouldn't affront Hannah's maid if she happened to glimpse him entering or leaving the pool, since he never wore a bathing suit. He stuffed the roll behind his neck and sighed at the stars.

He should have gone straight to bed, but he had come outside to feel closer to Hannah, as if coming home wasn't enough.

He had missed her while he was gone, much to his chagrin. And the baby, which was even more baffling. The most notice the boy had taken of him had been to curl a surprisingly firm grip around Akin's finger while half asleep. From what he'd observed, the infant did that with anyone who held him, so it was no great sign of affection, but Akin was looking forward to those tiny fingers holding him so trustingly again.

Pathetic.

He heard a soft noise and opened his eyes. There was flickering movement across the pool. Hannah's white wrap fluttered like an apparition as she slipped it on while weaving in and out of the moonlight and latticed shadows, making her way around the pool toward him.

He didn't move, wondering if he'd fallen asleep and was dreaming, because why would she come to him this way? She tied the light silk at her waist as she came around his end of the pool, but it did nothing to quell the free movement of her ample breasts or disguise their beautiful shape.

The banked fire in his blood flared and he dragged his gaze up to her faltering expression.

"Is the baby all right?" he asked.

"Sleeping. I just fed him and sent him back to his room, but I noticed you're back, so I came out to say hello." She crossed her arms as though regretting the impulse.

He cocked his head. "Am I wrong or does the dentist remain at the top of your Christmas list?"

Her white smile flashed briefly before she said, "The very tippy top."

"Let me see." He shifted his legs to the side a few inches and patted the space on the lounger beside his thigh.

She nervously lowered to the edge, tongue sliding across her teeth behind her lips, silk wrap tinted blue by the lights beneath the water.

"I thought you would be smiling nonstop."

"Like a crocodile, all day." She bared her teeth, then chuckled and ducked her chin. "But I've been trying to hide my teeth most of my life. Strangely enough, the braces felt like armor. I wasn't as self-conscious when I wore them, but now they're gone I'm back to thinking I can't let anyone see me smile."

"That would be a shame." He touched her wrist, enjoying her soft skin with a light caress, a strange tenderness rising in him as he regarded her. "It should be on your list. If you feel an urge to smile, smile."

A small one struggled to stick on her lips

while her gaze flickered to where he was touching her. She swallowed and he noted her nipples were jutting against the silk she wore.

Was making love on her list? He would add it to his own, he thought, as he brought her hand to his mouth. Lying with her would make him incredibly happy. He kissed the back of her knuckles then turned her hand so he could taste the thin skin inside her wrist, where her pulse was tripping so hard he felt it against his lips.

"I feel like I should tell you—" she blurted while her fingers flexed in reaction. "While you were gone, your mother said something that made think..."

Was there a more effective death knell for amorous thoughts than invoking a man's mother? He lowered her hand to the middle of his chest and waited.

She looked deeply uncomfortable. "It seemed very personal and I thought you would want to know that I...have an inkling your childhood might have been difficult."

His inner guardedness had relaxed at the sight of her, but it now clanked to attention, standing tall and ready to go on the offensive. He released her hand. "I don't want to talk about my childhood, Hannah."

"I don't expect you to." She tucked her hands between her knees, but the straight-up compassion in her tone landed on him like a lead blanket. She knew without him saying a damned thing. He could see it in her face, all soft with gentle concern.

It was the most exposed sensation he'd ever experienced. Like his throat was bared for a sword and his chest bared to a cannon. He rarely even acknowledged that old pain anymore, but she stood staring at it. *Seeing* it.

He held his breath, waiting to learn what she would do with her knowledge. With that weakness of his. That *flaw.*

"I hate talking about my childhood, too," she murmured, shifting her gaze to the pool so the lights threw ghostly shadows onto her face. "My mother died of a drug overdose and I didn't know anything about my father. My grandmother had a house, but only a tiny pension. I wore secondhand clothes and ate plain sandwiches in my lunch. I made them myself and did my own hair because of her arthritis. I didn't want to be a burden on her, but I was. All of that made me withdrawn. Libraries became my second home. I like learning, but libraries are a safe space too, where people have to behave. Other kids couldn't tease me or play jokes on me there."

He was going to build her a library, he decided.

"Grammy would tell me to just ignore them but pretending something doesn't affect you isn't the same as not being affected. She would also say things like, 'Bloom where you're planted.' You've done a good job of that." She tilted a shy smile at him. "I know you don't need to hear that. You know who you are. I admire that about you. It's something I want to become better at."

"Come here." He gathered her into his lap, not knowing how else to express himself. He didn't open himself the way she did. He only had this—action.

Her gaze flashed to his with surprise. "Don't feel sorry for me."

"I don't. I admire you, too." It was such a strong, sincere sentiment coming straight from his gut that it shook his heart on its way by.

Then he kissed her. Because this was the only way he knew how to let tenderness out of himself. She was lovely and pure and shockingly earnest, and she terrified him because she could be hurt so easily. How could he possibly protect her from the inevitable scrapes of existence? How could he protect her against himself?

Hannah didn't know how to kiss him back, not in a way that could compete with the way his mouth slayed her so completely. She felt utterly weak when his lips claimed hers so commandingly. Somehow he made her feel taken while giving so much, and she trembled under the intense feelings he provoked. The entire world stopped to hold them in a timeless place yet whirled so fast beyond them that she was dizzy.

In the back of her mind, she knew much of her reaction was infatuation. She couldn't help falling for a man who ticked all the alpha male boxes like great looks, money and power, but also had inner strength and a deep sense of loyalty that wasn't impacted by the injustices done to him.

The more she learned of him, the more she was humbled to be in his sphere. And she was *married* to him. Touching him. *Kissing* him. She would never measure up to all that he was, but she wanted to. She wanted to give him this same sense of being wanted that he invoked in her.

He couldn't know how deeply the heat of his hands moving on her back and the hardness of him against her hip thrilled her, but they did. She'd only been mocked for wanting love. For thinking compliments and caresses had been offered as heartfelt sentiments instead of a manipulation into the bedroom. This didn't feel like mockery, though. She cautioned herself against reading more than proximity into his desire, but it felt like genuine desire, which was enough.

He shifted her, deepening their kiss so his tongue pierced into her mouth, shooting a jolt of pleasure straight to her loins. She blatantly sucked on his tongue and he groaned. His big hand gathered her breast and he opened his thighs so her hip sank more firmly against the hard shape of him.

"I want to touch you everywhere, but I don't want to hurt you," he said against her mouth, then kissed her again with more head-spinning greed. "What can I do? Tell me."

"I want to touch *you*," she said, over-whelmed as it was. Letting him have his way with her would be too much—and maybe not enough. The little sex she'd experienced hadn't been as earth-shattering as she'd been led to believe. She didn't want that sort of disappointment between them, not when they were in such perfect accord right now. "Can I?"

"Touch me anywhere you like. I'm yours."

He wasn't. She knew better than to be-lieve that, but she wanted to. She wanted to claim him in ways she barely understood, but as he trailed his mouth into her neck, she pushed aside the edges of his robe and ran her hands across his pecs to find the sharp poke of his nipples.

She liked the way his chest swelled as he drew in a deep breath of reaction. It made her feel mighty and *equal*. She tilted so she could run her mouth to his nipples and lick around and across one then the other.

He hissed out a curse and his hand curled into her hair. "Let me do that to you."

She smiled against his skin and dabbed kisses down the trail of hair leading to his navel, opening his robe further as she went.

For all she'd lost in coming here, there were incredible things she'd gained and one of them was this. Him. He stunned her, this man who carried the weight of the world and was straining with arousal as she revealed him, but said, "You don't have to do that."

"I want to." She started to kneel and a rolled towel arrived to cushion her knees.

She barely noticed, too fascinated by the shape of him. With a tentative touch, she explored him. Kissed with parted lips, taking light tastes as she worked from the base of his shaft toward the tip.

His breath grew jagged. His stomach contracted. His foot fell off the far side of the lounger, opening his thighs so she had more room to caress him. She'd read about this more than she'd done it, but enthusiasm had to count for something? She closed her fist around the thickness of him and drew the velvety tip of him into her mouth.

"Hannah." His hand was on the back of her neck, not forcing her to take more. It was a reverent touch that moved into her hair, playing softly as she moved her mouth and tongue on him, discovering all the ways to make him twitch and stiffen and stop breathing altogether.

It was a magnificent experience. She loved how much *he* loved it. He was shaking, and when she lifted her lashes, she saw his eyes were on her, not closed and blocking her out as he drowned in what she was doing. His stare was alight with something fierce and hot as he watched her pleasure him. She could taste his growing excitement. Felt him swell to impossible hardness in her mouth.

"Stop," he said in a guttural voice.

No, she thought, but consent went both ways. She drew back, hurt, worried she'd done something wrong, but he closed his hand over hers and guided her fist to stroke. Once, twice—

Now his eyes closed and his head went back as he released a groan to the starry sky.

He pulsed strongly against her palm as he crushed her hand on himself in a way that ought to be painful, but...

But his gratification was so tangible she couldn't help her secretive smile. She had given him that and it had been a lot better than the blunt orgasm he'd given himself. She could tell.

He swiped the edge of his robe across his stomach, then gathered her into his lap. "Let me touch you. Give you that," he murmured as he nuzzled her cheek and the corner of her mouth.

"Can it just be this for now?"

"If that's what you want." He sounded drugged and slid a tickling caress across her shoulder and up to her nape. He tilted her head so he could kiss her, long and thorough. "Thank you."

She tucked her nose into his neck where he smelled divine and his pulse was still strong but slowing. His arms around her grew heavy and she knew he was falling asleep.

She was wide awake and tingling with arousal, but it felt nice to be cuddled, so she stayed exactly as she was, listening to his breaths settle into the slow, deep soughs of sleep.

She didn't realize she had also fallen asleep until he brushed her cheek and said, "*Ya amar.* The other man in your life needs you."

"Oh." The stars were gone and the sky pearlescent with coming dawn. With it came the realization she was lying on his mostly naked body out in the courtyard.

When she'd run her tongue all over him last night, she hadn't considered that she would have to make eye contact with him at some point. *Too soon!*

From the door to her apartment, she heard Qaswar's muted cry, as though the nanny was trying to appease him with his Binky or a bottle, but he knew what he wanted.

"I'll go." She stood so fast her head swam, and she nearly wobbled into the pool.

Behind her, she heard Akin leap to his feet, but she quickly got herself under control and hurried away.

CHAPTER EIGHT

NURA APOLOGIZED PROFUSELY for waking
Hannah, but Hannah hadn't even seen her.
She was too befuddled and embarrassed to
do more than brush the whole thing off, as-
suring Nura she'd done the right thing.

Hannah pumped for emergencies, but
she had made very clear to all the staff that
she preferred to breastfeed her son even if
it meant waking her. She only wished she
hadn't fallen asleep so soundly, forcing
Nura to come out. The poor woman had
only wanted to gently shake her awake, but
whatever she'd seen in Akin's eyes when he
snapped them open had spooked Nura into
believing he wished her staked on an anthill.

Hannah tried to reassure the girl that Akin
wouldn't have been upset in any way, but
she suspected Nura was as relieved as she
was when the only word they had from him

that day was the message that he would like Hannah to continue visiting his mother in his stead.

Hannah was a tiny bit stung but reasoned that he had just returned after being away two weeks and would have a lot of work to catch up on. She wasn't ready to talk to him, anyway. Going out to greet him, she'd only been seeking a chat, not...*that.*

Then the pearls arrived. The necklace was like an infinity scarf that could be twisted and turned into drapes of three or four or five strings. Nura was thrilled and couldn't wait to try all the clasps and pendants so she could rehearse a full repertoire of styles, but Hannah was appalled. Was he sending her some sort of *reward* for what she'd done?

Akin hadn't included a note and, as two more days of silence passed, Hannah made a couple of discreet inquiries about the King. He hadn't taken a sudden downturn, so that left Akin's reason for ignoring her a mystery.

As her hurt and pique grew, Hannah decided she would rather not hear from him. There was no way she was reaching out to him, either. Not when he was ghosting her worse than a frat boy who'd passed his final and no longer needed a free tutor. Been there, done that, and made all the poor excuses for jerks who didn't deserve her benefit of the doubt in the first place.

On day five after their encounter by the pool, she arrived at his mother's parlor to find him there. He wore the green robe that usually meant he'd been with foreign dignitaries, and looked as though he'd had a fresh beard trim. He stopped whatever he was saying to swing his attention to her.

Damn him and his bedroom eyes. She hated that the sight of him made her feel as though a wave picked her up and tried to float her toward him.

"Oh, you're here. How nice," she forced herself to say, as she handed the baby to Tadita. She didn't show her teeth when she stretched her lips in a flat smile and sent it in Akin's general direction. "I'll leave you to your family time."

"Hannah," he said in *that* tone, the one that instructed missiles to launch or armies to halt.

It hit her in the middle of her spine, but

she ignored it. She ignored him *hard* as she stalked away with her eyes on fire.

He didn't come after her, which was even more insulting than if he had caught up to her and chewed her out in public.

Maybe she was overreacting, she cautioned herself as her belly churned with misgiving. She lived in her own bubble here. Perhaps the zombie apocalypse was in full swing and Akin had been tied up with digging a moat around Baaqi. Perhaps zombies choked on pearls and that was why he'd sent them instead of a note that said something like, *I'll be tied up for a few days and will call as soon as I'm free.*

There could be any number of rational explanations for his ignoring her, but letting a man treat her like garbage was not on her happiness list.

Prince Akin could go to hell and he was *not* taking her with him.

Akin probably should have checked the palace library first. He probably should have read into the fact that she'd *gone* to the library, and not have entered the hallowed space the way a bull entered a china shop.

However, by the time he had sat with his mother, explained that the "white nanny" was actually his wife, been berated *again* for marrying the mother of Eijaz's son, he was already aggravated. And he'd walked all the way across the palace to discover Hannah hadn't returned to her rooms—suffering a stark moment of panic when he thought she'd gone missing, even as her bodyguard took his own sweet time to reveal her whereabouts. *Then* he'd paced all the way across the palace again to the library, his patience thinning to its very last thread.

"Out," he barked to the cavernous room, startling a handful of clerics and Hannah, who lifted her nose from a book she was browsing near a shelf on the upper gallery.

She gave him one very haughty look, then slid her book back onto the shelf and came down the stairs with her gaze on the door, as if she was calmly exiting during a fire drill.

"Not you," he said. "And you damned well know it."

She stopped on the bottom step, one hand

on the top of the post. "You're supposed to talk quietly in a library," she reminded him stiffly as the door closed behind the last straggler.

"I don't have time for games, Hannah. Ever. If we have a problem, let's confront it and get through it."

Her fist closed on the post, the only sign that she wasn't comfortable with facing conflict head-on. "I find gifts for sex insulting."

Wow. She might not be comfortable with fighting, but she didn't pull her punches when she decided to throw some.

"That's not what it was. I knew I wouldn't see you for—"

"I don't care." She spoke over him. "I don't care what you thought you were saying by sending it. It came across as paying me for sex. That's gross. If you want to say something to me, do what you're forcing me to do and say it to my face. Don't encode it. I'm not going to guess. Obviously, mistakes can be made," she summed up tightly.

Anyone else would understand what a land mine they stood on, talking to him like this.

Not Hannah. She was as infuriatingly magnificent in her temper as ever.

It was moments like this that had imprinted her on his thoughts. He'd been reliving their intimate encounter almost continuously. She had leveled him, virtually leaving him in a coma. Which was one of the reasons he hadn't made a point of seeking her out right away. For those exquisite minutes, she had been his entire world. It was humbling to realize how helpless he'd been while she'd caressed him with her mouth. His climax had been incredible. He'd succumbed to such a deep sleep afterward, her maid had been on the point of touching Hannah's shoulder to wake her before his awareness of the young woman's approach had penetrated his consciousness.

He typically slept very lightly. *No one* surprised him.

Whatever had been in Akin's eyes when he snapped awake to see a shadow reaching for his wife had sent the maid running back in terror to Hannah's chambers.

Everything had added up to a level of vulnerability that disturbed him. Akin didn't allow himself weaknesses. Softness and distractions got a man killed. Caring was a one-way endeavor that ultimately left him empty.

"You know I have many demands on my time. I've made that clear," he reminded.

"And you understand that my desire to have a baby alone was for this reason right here. I don't want to expect anything from a man. I *don't* expect anything from you," she insisted, voice growing strident. "I won't, in future anyway. And you shouldn't expect anything from me. What happened the other night will never happen again."

A clammy hand folded around his entire being. "We're married," he said grittily, as if that had anything to do with anything.

"It's not a real marriage. You've made that more than clear, as well."

He stepped forward into the fray, as he would to rescue anything that was important to him.

She stepped back, stumbling slightly on the step above the one she stood on. She caught her balance with a hand on the wall behind her and pressed her back firmly against it.

As insults went, that retreat was one of the most cutting she could deliver.

"I'm never going to hurt you, Hannah."

"But you did!" She leaned into that accusation, pointing at him. "I thought you were starting to like me. That you kissed me because you wanted us to be more than allies. We agreed not to lie to one another and what you let happen was a *lie*."

He was not the romantic young fool he'd once been. That was what he'd been telling himself these last few days as he fought the craving that had begun to eat at him from the moment Hannah disappeared into her chambers.

"I'm not like you, Akin. My self-esteem is an eggshell. Every man I was ever involved with stepped all over me. They acted like they wanted to be with me, but they only wanted to copy my homework or tell their friends they got the frigid librarian to give it up. They were mean and they *didn't care*. You should have warned me that you were *just like them*."

As fights went, he was taking the beating of his life. His ears rang, amplifying the injured tone in her words. And he wanted to kill those other men. Actually erase them from this earth.

"Where is the man who keeps telling me it's his duty to protect Qaswar's mother from harm?" she charged.

"I was trying to protect you," he ground out. Both of them, really, but he'd gone about it backward. He saw that with blinding clarity now.

"By running hot and cold? Thanks," she scoffed derisively, tears standing on her lashes.

Akin scowled into the middle distance, heart pounding. He ran a hand down his face.

"I'm not like those men. I do like you." He hated to revisit the past, but he could see it was necessary so she would understand why his ignoring her had made twisted sense to him. "But I was in love once."

Her breath hissed in as though he was the one who'd landed a blow. It only made him feel worse as she stood there so white-lipped and injured.

"Perhaps it was infatuation. That's what I

was told it was." He spilled the words dispassionately so he wouldn't dwell on the layers that went beyond a bruised heart to profound scorn from the people who were supposed to love him. "We were young, but I wanted to marry her. I knew I was expected to wait until Eijaz married, then accept the bride my mother chose for me. I planned an elopement anyway. My father sent me into the desert on a mission that kept me there for months. When I emerged, she was married and living in Australia. They have two daughters. I've heard she's very happy, so I suppose we weren't in love. Still, I'm careful about revealing where my affections might lie."

"You thought someone would put me on a ship to the colonies if you treated me with an ounce of respect?"

"I don't know, do I?" he snapped. He had his own back to a wall, and he *hated* it. "I still have a king who has the power to make brutal decisions without regard to how they affect me. I have been soundly schooled on that, Hannah. My feelings have never mattered. If I let *you* matter beyond the duty I have toward you and your son…"

He didn't want to finish that sentence. He didn't want to contemplate any scenario where this very nascent thing between them was snatched away and given to someone else.

"That's how you made me feel." Hannah's subdued voice seemed to fill the empty room. "Like I don't matter. It doesn't help that you're saying you fell in love once and wouldn't dare take that risk again."

"You do matter," he growled. "I should have made that more than clear to everyone, including you. I see that now. My mother thinks you're the damned nanny and I've allowed that to go on because…" He waved a hand.

Some of the starch left Hannah's shoulders. "I don't care about that," she mumbled.

"*I* care, Hannah. I just don't have the ability to change her mind." He'd never had, and these days her mind was next to impossible to reach, let alone fix. "I can't be seen as trying to snatch power from my dead brother and weak father, either." He sighed, exhausted by a sense of futility. "I've been holding off on taking any bold steps until…"

"The ceremony." She had hold of her own elbows.

"Yes." The official handoff from King to Regent wouldn't happen for another two months. "You had enough on your plate with the move and having a new baby. The press was all over you. I thought keeping you tucked out of the way was in your best interest. I see now that it's not."

"What does *that* mean?" She seemed to try to blend into the striped wallpaper.

"It means it is time for you to take your public position as the mother of Baaqi's future king. As my wife. You'll stand at my side as I go about my duties and my people will see by my regard and respect for you that I'm caretaking our country, not taking it. They'll recognize your value and protect you as I do."

"No, they won't! They hate me!"

"Who does?"

"Trolls," she said with an abstract lift of her arm. "All those people who were saying things online. The press."

"*Were.* They aren't anymore. I've forbidden it."

"Pfft! I should have thought of doing that myself! They stopped because I've been hiding, Akin. Leave me tucked away. I'm sorry I said anything."

"No. This is the right thing to do. You'll see."

"You are *so wrong.*"

"Hannah."

"Don't use that tone on me. I don't like it."

"Hannah," he said as gently as he could, while closing in on her.

She shook her head and the scarf over her head was dislodged because she was still trying to disappear through the solid wall at her back.

He set his hands on the wall on either side of her shoulders, liking that she was up on a step, because it brought her high enough her eyes were even with his mouth. He wasn't bullying or intimidating her. They *were* equals.

"You will not ask to be ignored, because you just told me that it hurt you when I did that to you," he pointed out.

"That was because…" Her bottom lip wasn't quite steady. The heel of her hand pressed the hollow of his shoulder.

"You thought I didn't respect you. I do. We are more than allies."

Her gaze flashed up to his.

"We're partners," he said.

Her lashes swept down again to hide whatever came into her eyes at that.

"You will not run from me or anyone who sees you as less than you are, because you are not a coward. Look who you are standing up to right now."

"Is that what I'm doing?" Her hand was more resting than resisting, but he wasn't pushing into her space, either.

He wanted to, though. He wanted to flatten her to the wall and feel every soft curve cushion him. He wanted to run his hands over her, his mouth…

He wanted to take because, "I'm not used to being given things," he confessed. "I've trained myself not to want anything, but suddenly the world is in my lap."

Literally. Her in his lap the other night had

brought on the most profound rest he'd experienced in years.

"I'm taking my brother's place as father and ruler. His *son* is mine. Pleasure of any kind has always been a fleeting thing to me. Incidental. Yet you gave it to me with such selflessness." He grazed her cheekbone with the pad of his thumb. "I didn't know how to accept it gracefully. I still don't. But I want this marriage to be a real one. I want *you*, Hannah. It's not comfortable for me to admit that."

Her brow gave a little flex of agony and he set his mouth there, trying to ease whatever hurt he was causing, because it was the last thing he wanted to do.

Hannah didn't know if she was being the biggest fool alive, falling for a line, or reaching for salvation when she let her hand slowly slide up from Akin's shoulder until her arm was twined around his neck.

Akin seemed to shudder as she stretched against him and let him take her weight as she came off the wall, but she thought she might be trembling, so it was hard to tell which one of them shook. Either way, he wrapped both his arms around her, drawing her into his embrace, and the shaken feeling between them became mutual.

At the same time, he felt warm and solid and secure. Safe. Maybe it was because she was at such a close height to him. She felt like she might be able to handle him right then. Almost. Because as she drew her head back to look at him, he swooped to capture her mouth.

If she had doubted his claim that he wanted her, she had her proof here in the greed of his kiss. Not selfish—oh, no—but hungry and thorough. The control that was so much a part of him was gone as he cradled the back of her head and devoured her lips and swept his tongue into her mouth.

It was overwhelming and might have left her hanging weakly off him another time, but a hot, brilliant need flashed alive inside her, one that wanted him just as fiercely. A dim voice warned caution way in the back of her head, but she ignored it in favor of catching her fist in the back of his collar and clashing her tongue against his.

He groaned and backed her into the wall again. Her foot caught again, and she would have stumbled, but he was right there, so steady, anchoring her to this world even as she spun off to a new one. Their mouths parted and crashed together again and again in a mindless gluttony that was pure hedonism.

She forgot where they were, who they were. All that mattered was his mouth and the silken scrape of his beard against her chin, the scent of him drugging her senses and the feel of his hair between her fingers as she got under his kaffiyeh, dislodging the cord that held the headdress in place, so the square of cotton slid away.

Her scarf was long gone, brushed away by busy hands that roamed from her hair to her shoulder, down to her ribs and her backside and up to her waist and splayed over her breasts so she danced and twisted into his touch every which way, thinking, *more. More.*

When his mouth trailed into her neck and his clever fingers drew down the zip of her abaya, she only sighed in relief at the rush of cool air that wafted into her cleavage.

"What the hell are you wearing?" He pushed it open to reveal her sport bra and yoga shorts topped by a loose tank.

"I've been going to the gym after visiting your mother." There was an all-women Zumba class she liked. She had thought to bide her time in the library today, rather than go all the way back to her chambers. Sometimes abayas were superconvenient since no one knew what she wore underneath, but what she was wearing right now, that Akin was seeing, made her feel really self-conscious of the fact she was showing a lot of skin. "I still have baby weight." On curves that had been pretty curvy in the first place.

"In all the right places." He gave her thigh a gentle squeeze, then sent his palm on a slow circle over her butt cheek before grabbing a handful and making a noise of satisfaction. "You're incredibly sexy, Hannah."

She wasn't. He was being kind, but she would take it. Although she said, "We probably shouldn't do this here."

"Do what?" His mouth was nipping and

nibbling along her jaw while his fingertips traced along the edge of her tight shorts, teasing the exposed skin of her upper thighs. "This is your happy place, isn't it? Let me make you happy."

She choked on a laugh since his hand was traveling up the inside of her thigh to cup her mound.

"I—I couldn't," she gasped as his lips found a spot on her neck that weakened her knees.

"No? Let's try."

"That wasn't what I meant." She unconsciously tried to squeeze her thighs together, mostly in reaction because she had never been very comfortable with being touched so intimately. This was different, though. This was Akin and, if anything, she was trying to slow him down so she could think, but he was taking his time anyway.

"Hannah." Sometimes the way he said her name made it sound pure and divine. "Accept this gracefully." He drew a light touch with his fingertips, up and down. The tightness of her shorts accentuated the sensation so hot tingles rushed into the flesh he caressed.

She quivered and a sob sounded in her throat.

"Where are my earrings, *ya amar*?" He sucked on her earlobe and cupped her again, this time firm as he began to rock his hand.

"W-what?"

"You're so hot here. Move with me. Show me how you like it." His mouth came back to hers and he kissed her passionately, encouraging her to rock against his firm hand.

It wouldn't work, but it felt good and she wanted to keep doing it. She'd only had about a million fantasies that involved being seduced in a library, so she kept moving, but it wouldn't work because she was too repressed to give herself over to anyone.

Still, when Akin abruptly stopped, she could have screamed in panicked frustration. He slid his hand upward, though, under the edge of her tank to caress the skin of her midriff, then he slid his fingers under the tight waistband of her shorts. He struggled to work his hand back down within the confines of the spandex.

She caught her breath, thinking she should tell him not to bother, but she held very still, paralyzed by the glitter of heat in his dark eyes. When his fingertips found her slippery folds, she jolted.

"*So* hot," he breathed against her lips as his fingertips did wicked, magical things, moving incrementally against the constrictive fabric, but with untold power. "I keep thinking of the way you looked when you had your mouth on me. I want to do that to you. Make you orgasm so hard you pass out."

"I—I—" She had no words. *Don't watch me*, she wanted to plead, because despite how flagrant this was, she was thinking now about how he had hardened in her mouth—

Two firm fingers right *there*. Like he was pushing a button. She had her hand over his, trapping his hand in her shorts as she lifted her hips into his touch and closed her eyes, moving against his fingertips as she succumbed to a sharp orgasm that rocked her loins. It was so strong it made her breasts hurt and her womb contract while luscious waves of pleasure engulfed her.

She knew she was making noises of abandonment that echoed to the high ceiling and she didn't care because it felt *so good*.

His voice rumbled words she couldn't understand, and his lips were teasing her ear and neck and stealing kisses while she shuddered and gasped and very slowly came down from standing on her toes.

They kissed passionately, but even though she gave him her tongue, he began to withdraw. His hand left her shorts and he made a noise of reluctance as he steered her touch from the firm shape she found through the layers of his clothes.

"I would say we are even now, but you still owe me one," he teased to soften his rebuff. "We'll revisit this later. I'll dine with you."

And that was it, she realized. All the cards were falling.

She *was* a fool. A bigger fool than she'd ever been with any other man. Those past crushes of hers had been experiments and attempts to find a like-minded companion and accept sex in place of the sincere regard she longed for.

This was completely different. This man

now had a hold on her in a thousand subtle ways. She didn't just want him to like her and be friends with her. She wanted to *deserve* him. She wanted to make *him* happy. She wanted to gift herself over to him and yearned for him to do the same for her.

She was falling in love with him and he had just told her he was afraid to let her matter. He had trained himself not to want anything.

He might not be like those men who had hurt her in the past, but he could definitely hurt her in the future, and she had no defenses left against him.

CHAPTER NINE

WHEN AKIN DECIDED to take bold steps, he took them in bounding strides that left Hannah breathless, trying to keep up.

He dined with her that day and held his nephew, kissed the hell out of her and apologized when phone calls forced him to disappear for the rest of the evening.

She had half expected to be ignored again, but first thing next morning, while she was still eating her grapefruit and slice of toast, she received a message that she should meet him at his offices across the palace.

Nura, bless her, put Hannah in a flowing pantsuit that was trendy and smart, yet demure enough that she was perfectly attired for her meet and greets with armies of staff.

Akin was by her side through all of it, keeping things short and on task, reminding everyone she had a new baby so would only work a few hours a day, but he made it clear Hannah would gradually take on all of the Queen's previous duties.

"I don't actually know how to be a queen—you know that, right?" Hannah said when she finally had him alone in *her* office.

It was a stunning space with an adorable neoclassical French decor, built-in shelves she could pack with books, and abundant natural light from the doors to the balcony that overlooked the palace gardens.

"Did you know how to be a mother before you became one?"

"Oh. Same level of life-and-death stakes if I screw up, I presume?"

"See, you're a natural."

"Please don't make light. I'm terrified." She opened a door and interrupted a half dozen worker bees setting up workstations for her new battalion of assistants. They froze and looked expectantly at her. "Sorry," she muttered and closed it again. At least she would only be taking meetings in the palace at first and mostly in organizational capacities. "When do I have to, like, be in public with you?"

"How do you define 'public'? We're hosting a dinner tonight."

"Tonight! No, we're not. For whom?"

"Neighboring royalty. Kings who are allies and have a lot of influence, as do their wives. You'll like them."

Wives. Oh, dear God. How could he be so smart, yet so dumb?

"Your maid will show you to the harem once they've arrived—"

"You have a *harem*?"

"What do you think a harem is, Hannah? Sex slaves in a genie bottle? It's a set of rooms for female visitors so they have as much privacy as they desire. Their husbands have accommodation in the same wing if they'd rather sleep with them, but there is space for servants and children if they bring them. It's convenience and culture, not dictate. Greeting them there will allow you to visit in a casual setting before dinner. I'll do the same with the husbands in my private lounge."

She shoved her fists under her elbows. "Can I take Qaswar?"

"As a human shield?"

"People like babies."

"Hannah."

"Don't tell me I'm not a coward." She jerked her chin away from the light hand that tried to force her to look at him. "You be the girl in middle school with acne and the wrong label on her jeans, then tell me how brave *you* would be, walking into a room full of *queens*. This was never part of our deal, Akin."

He took hold of her fists and unbent her arms, trying to lever her closer.

"No. You don't get a kiss." She turned her face away. "I'm mad at you. You sprang this on me without any warning."

"This is your warning. I didn't invite them until yesterday, after our talk in the library." His mouth twitched on the word "talk." She gave her fists a shake, trying to get him to release her, but he only slid his hands up her arms, keeping her before him. "They confirmed this morning and now I'm telling you we have an engagement. Take Qaswar if you want to, but you won't need him."

He drew her close, but she stayed stiff as a board, determined to convey her displeasure, but he ran his magic hands over her, and she began to melt.

"You can sleep with your husband, you know. Come to my room. We don't have to meet like teenagers sneaking out at night."

"You're never there. Are you?"

"I haven't had a reason to make getting to bed a priority. Have I?" he countered.

She would have her post-childbirth checkup in a couple of days and be ready for what he seemed to have in mind, but she ducked her head, not prepared to contemplate how thoroughly he could destroy her with an all-night seduction.

"This is a lot of performance anxiety to put on me all at once."

"Yesterday was a 'performance'? Let's have an encore." He started to back her toward a desk where his mother had sat for decades, signing checks for charities and answering letters.

Thankfully, there was a ping from her new tablet.

"The other man in my life needs me." She patted his chest and made her escape.

* * *

Hannah very miserably put on a floral dress that would be awful to nurse in and a pair of heeled shoes that rubbed her ankle. Nura did her makeup and draped a light scarf over hair that had grown out to midway between pixie and bob.

At least her son was pretty. He took after his father, with his dark eyes and black hair and thick, curling lashes that belonged on a supermodel. Which made him resemble his uncle, not that Hannah had spent much time mooning over *that*.

Nura accompanied her along with a nanny to a section of the palace Hannah had never been. A handful of bodyguards stood outside an unassuming door but let her pass after briefly checking their screens to ensure she was who she claimed to be.

Hannah walked into what looked like a boutique hotel. There was a desk where one of the palace assistants sat to greet them. Beyond it, there was a hallway with a half dozen doors and stairs and an elevator. On the other side was a small dining lounge with doors that opened onto a private courtyard smaller than her own, but similar.

Through the glass, Hannah saw three women sitting at a table. Nura had coached her that the one with typical Arab coloring was Galila, Queen of Zyria. The ivory-skinned redhead was Fern, an Englishwoman who had become Queen of Q'Amara, and the brunette was Angelique, Queen of Zhamair.

They were talking over each other and laughing, clearly familiar and comfortable with one another. They all wore casual western day dresses like Hannah's but somehow looked incredibly beautiful and relaxed while Hannah felt like a prickly frump.

She wanted to cry, she really did, but the wretched greeter hurried to announced her.

"May I present to you the Crown Prince of Baaqi and his mother, Princess Hannah?"

All the women stopped talking and stood up with an air of expectation as she came outside. Hannah forced a smile.

"Welcome to Baaqi. I hope you've settled in? Please call me Hannah."

They introduced themselves. Galila was pregnant and made it look effortless. All of them cooed over the baby and begged to hold him.

No, he's mine, Hannah wanted to growl but had to say a gracious "Of course."

Fern had two older sons who were elsewhere, but her four-month-old daughter came out moments later, having freshly woken. She had black hair and two small teeth and came to Hannah with a big smile.

Babies, Hannah discovered, made for very good icebreakers. And great equalizers. They all had questions for one another and stories of their misadventures as new moms.

When Angelique talked about all the twins in her family, Hannah realized she hadn't recognized her famous guest—the first of what she assumed would be her many faux pas for the evening.

"Forgive me. I didn't make the connection. You're one of the Sauveterre twins! You and your sister had the design house. You must think me an idiot for not putting it together."

"We still own it. We just don't get to do as much of the actual work as we used to. It turns out motherhood is a full-time job. Who knew?" she said with facetious humor.

Somehow an hour passed, and Hannah discovered she was as comfortable as if she had joined a handful of librarians to talk shop in the break room. She had forgotten she wasn't one of them, but as Galila excused herself to lie down before dinner, Hannah realized she still had an entire evening—the rest of her life, in fact—to get through.

"May I ask you both something?" Hannah ventured after Galila left. "I know you've spent a lot of your life in the public eye, and I wondered if you've struggled with all the publicity?"

"You mean when my husband got his nieces' governess pregnant out of wedlock? It was a cake walk," Fern said in her dry British accent. "Karim's mother was terrified for my life, so *that* helped."

"Oh. I'm so sorry. I'm not facing that, I don't think. I'm just worried about online haters. They've already had a go at me, but it died down while I was out of the spotlight. Now Akin wants me to start making appearances and…" She hated admitting she was a target. It felt too much like admitting she deserved it, but she had to voice her need.

"I wondered if you had any advice on coping. I dread what they might say."

"You know what they say about haters," Angelique remarked. *"Nothing."*

Fern's laughter bubbled up and Hannah snickered, as well.

"I can't take credit for that," Angelique confided. "It's my sister's, but she was treated horribly for *years*." Angelique's gaze dimmed with introspection and her jaw set. Her phone buzzed and she smiled. "There she is, wondering what's wrong." She tapped a heart and set the phone aside. "It's awful that people think they can behave that way. All you can do is remind yourself that the things they say aren't true."

"But what if they are?" Hannah asked faintly.

"What do you mean?" Angelique had the most compassionate eyes Hannah had ever seen. She was so beautiful it was intimidating, yet there was an incredible softness to her that made it possible for Hannah to reveal her darkest hurt.

"I'm…" She stopped short of saying *ugly*. "Not pretty."

"Hannah." Angelique turned in her chair and picked up her hands. "I'm going to say to you what I've said to my own sister. If you feel down on yourself, if you feel bloated or you have a spot or some other thing that makes you feel less than beautiful, that's okay. Your feelings are yours and I'm not going to tell you not to feel them. And if a stranger says something that hurts you, your hurt is valid. But they're *trying* to hurt you. That's not honesty. It's cruelty. Believing what they say is like believing you would deserve it if they hit you. They're not the type of people you would admire or respect if you met them, so please don't give more weight to their remarks than the things said by people who care about you."

"I—" Hannah had to take back one of her hands to press her trembling lips. She'd been struggling to believe she had anyone who cared about her here. What she really feared, deep down, was that Akin would believe those remarks and realize what a mistake he'd made. "I know I shouldn't let their opinions matter so much, but it feels so much like the truth. I've never felt pretty," she confessed with wet eyes.

"Angelique made me cry the first time we met, too," Fern said, rubbing her shoulder.

"I know in my head it shouldn't matter how I look," Hannah continued. "I'm never going to be tall and skinny, but when I look in the mirror, I don't see 'pretty' and that makes it feel as though what people say is true."

"When I look in a mirror, I see my sister, so I always love what I see," Angelique said wryly. "But the things that make me feel pretty are things I can literally feel. Soft fabric and my hair loose on my shoulders. Laughing. Showing my husband my new lingerie." She cast her gaze to the sky, making them chuckle. "But I did make a career in helping women feel confident and beautiful. You have incredible skin, Hannah. And nursing mothers have a built-in advantage. Look at Fern making the most of what's she's got."

"Use them 'til you lose them." Fern sat taller, straining the buttons on her bodice.

"What are you wearing tonight?" Angelique asked. "Can I come help you get ready?"

"Do a makeover?" Hannah shook her head. "It would look like I'm trying too hard."

"You don't need to be anything but who you are," Angelique said firmly. "You're perfect. But I miss playing dress-up with my sister. It's great bonding time and I *do* know a few tricks that might help you feel you're getting the most from your wardrobe. Please?"

The word "bonding" got her. She needed friends, so she nodded, hoping Nura would be able to tone things down if Angelique went too far.

Fern elected to stay back and call her sons, so Hannah promised to see her at dinner and nervously brought Angelique back to her apartment.

Akin believed in diplomacy over combat, which wasn't to say he wouldn't resort to combat if it came to that. Tonight was meant to be ambassadorial, but there was every chance his actions would be seen as aggressive. They were definitely tactical.

He had invited three of the most powerful

kings in his region for an unofficial meeting he had billed as a social opportunity to introduce his wife to theirs. None of them were stupid. They knew more was afoot or they would have had more notice.

To call them friends would be an overstatement. They were traditional allies and all well acquainted from years of attending weddings and funerals, coronations and the occasional crossing of paths near a desert border.

They were also circumspect men who would make up their own minds. Whatever opinions they shared outside the palace after this visit would carry a great deal of weight around the globe.

After tonight, Baaqi would either be seen as vulnerable, with a weakened king and no confirmed ruler, or in steady hands with Akin at the helm.

Akin brought each man into his father's chamber to briefly pay his respects, king to king. His father's ill health and lack of interest in continuing to reign was painfully obvious.

Afterward, they all convened with drinks

in a private lounge reserved for mingling with exalted guests such as they were.

"Take heed, men," Zafir said as they clinked glasses. "Our fathers stood like this at one time and thought they would be our age forever."

"We should be so lucky as to enjoy a long life," Karim said. Both he and Zafir had lost their fathers when they were young.

"It's sobering to confront mortality at any time," Kasim agreed with introspection. "I'm reminded of my own father in his later years. The delicate tightrope that has to be walked."

It was an acknowledgment of the difficult position Akin was in, finding the balance between his father's right to rule, his regal pride, and the fact he simply no longer had the capacity to do it.

"It's an equally difficult balance to be the uncle who raises a king," Karim said with a nod of acknowledgment to Akin that was also a subtle warning. "Mine was much like you. A firm, steady influence who modeled the devotion to duty I've carried with me to this day."

We know what you're doing, Karim was saying. *We're watching and can make things uncomfortable internationally if we don't like what we see.*

"At least you were old enough to have learned basic manners," Akin said dryly. "I held Qaswar the other day when he visited my mother and walked around the rest of the day wondering, what is that smell?"

"Ah. The bewitching aroma of new father. I'm likely wearing it myself," Zafir said with a grimacing glance at his own shoulder.

They chuckled and moved on to discussing other matters, but Akin knew he was still on trial. If Qaswar had not existed, Akin would have been recognized as the rightful heir and allowed to take control without question.

He was not, though. There was a baby who held that title and these men wanted reassurances this was not a power-grab that could destablize the entire region. They would bring their own armies to stand behind the infant against Akin if it came to it. Without their support, Akin had nothing.

Which was why he needed to push Hannah into the spotlight, despite her voiced reluctance to be anywhere near it. Until Qaswar was old enough, she was the placeholder to whom Akin would demonstrate his dedication. It was a play to reassure the public, but it was sincere. Ironically, his life would be so much more straightforward if Qaswar hadn't existed, but Akin couldn't find any regret in him that the boy did.

A subtle knock announced the women were joining them.

Akin suffered a moment of concern. If Hannah walked in looking hurt and ill used, he would have to take a completely different tack, starting with banishing any catty queens who had dared to claw at his little mouse. She might not be the most glamorous wom—

As the hostess, Hannah led the parade of graceful beauties and Akin's mouth went dry as she moved with assurance among them. *As one of them.*

His heart swelled with such pride he could barely see over his chest.

They all wore long dinner gowns. Hannah's was bronze and poured down her voluptuous figure like caramel syrup over ice cream. It offered a generous view of her upper chest and coated her hips, puddling in a small train behind her. Her hair had been trimmed and reshaped into a smooth cap and was topped by a small tiara that leant her an air of quiet sophistication.

Her glasses were gone, her lashes decidedly false, but her smile was genuine and so filled with confidence that he was utterly dazzled. She wore heels and came across to him with a roll of her hips that was every man's wet dream.

"My wife. Princess Hannah," he introduced as she arrived at his side. He wanted to throw her over his shoulder and take her somewhere private to ravage her. For *days*.

She greeted each man in turn with a personal comment. "Your daughter is so precious. I'm hoping Fern can coach me on how to raise such a happy baby… Galila was telling me about your country's literacy endeavors. I'm looking forward to stealing all her inspired ideas… Thank you for loaning me Angelique this afternoon. She's been so generous and has been enduring my practice of very rusty Spanish."

Every single one of the men managed to keep his eyes on her smile, but Akin knew that despite the fact that each was completely enamored with his own very beautiful wife, they all noted Hannah's loveliness. Any male with a pulse would.

He experienced a surprisingly deep stab of possessiveness as he perceived it and closed his hand over hers in a blatant claim that was a betrayal of his inner barbarian. Not like him at all to feel it or reveal it, but he couldn't stop himself.

They all chatted a little longer before moving into the small dining room, where a square table put each couple on a side so as not to put a prince above a king, even though Akin was the host.

"No glasses?" Akin murmured as he seated Hannah.

"Contacts. That's why I'm blinking like a first-class flirt."

She was and it was adorable. Probably the sexiest thing she did, however, was reveal how incredibly intelligent she was. As conversation meandered from mild gossip about a scandal at the boarding school Zafir's son attended to complex political issues, Hannah listened attentively, asking incisive questions and offering smart, fresh perspective.

It was the most relaxed and genuinely social evening Akin had experienced in recent memory. When the women rose to retire for the night, they kissed each other's cheeks and promised reciprocal invitations soon. Akin would have dismissed it as a meaningless courtesy, but their husbands backed them up.

"We're in England next month, but will you accompany Akin when he attends our trade forum in June?" Zafir asked with a glance at Akin, who nodded. "I'll arrange rooms for you at the palace."

Akin had rooms booked at the hotel where all the meetings would be held, which would be more convenient for him, but this was the seal of approval he'd sought with tonight's dinner, so he said, "Thank you. We'd be honored."

Hannah wouldn't say that she magically felt beautiful and confident and fit to be a queen after eating dinner with royalty, but she did feel less of an imposter after spending the day with those women.

Galila had been raised a princess, but even though she looked amazing, and wore the title of Queen without any seeming effort, she'd confessed that pregnancy had taken a toll. Hannah had very much identified with that.

And how could she not relate to Fern, a single mother's daughter with education her only real asset, who had accidentally become pregnant by a man with royal blood?

Then Angelique had been so warm and encouraging and an absolute genius about the colors and styles that best suited Hanna's figure. The whole evening had gone so well that Hannah was unable to focus on anything but the positives.

It had added up to the boost she needed to step into the role Akin demanded of her. Well, the public role, anyway. She had since held a tea for a handful of chairwomen running charities the Queen sponsored, and had accompanied Akin to a ground-breaking for what would eventually be Baaqi's parliament buildings.

Her private role as his wife was making her wring her hands with nerves, though.

She hadn't actually seen her husband since the night with the royals. A land use dispute at an oil field had taken him away for two nights and he'd been up early this morning, texting that he was needed in his office and couldn't breakfast with her, but…

Come by my office on your way to yours.

She did, but even though things had been going really well between them, butterflies invaded her stomach when she heard his voice as she was shown through the catacomb of offices occupied by his assistants and advisers and approached the one that was his.

It was an imposing room that reflected his military service in its ruthlessly practical decor. A handful of dignitaries were leaving so there were introductions all around before she was left with only him and two of his assistants, both anxious to pour water, slant the blinds so the light wasn't in her eyes, hold her chair and fetch cake and coffee if she so desired?

"I'm perfectly comfortable, thank you," Hannah assured them.

"Close the door on your way out," Akin ordered dryly.

Hannah waited until they'd done so before brushing her scarf off her hair. "Far be it from me to complain, but you may have made *too* big a deal about their giving me every consideration."

"No one offers *me* sweetcakes with my coffee," he grumbled.

"Because they know you eat the hearts of your enemies with your morning coffee."

"I'll eat certain sweetcakes." His hungry look was not an appetite for food. "If they have a sprinkle of spice."

"Flirt," she accused, blushing as she looked to the closed blinds.

"You started it, coming in here with that chic haircut that makes me want to muss it up. How much longer do we have to wait, *ya amar*? Did you see the doctor while I was away?"

"Yes." She had an urge to open the neck of

her blouse and let some of the heat against her throat escape. "He gave me an IUD and said it's effective immedia—"

Akin hit a button on his desk. A distant buzzer sounded and the door promptly opened. A young man poked his head in. *"Sayidi?"*

"Clear both our schedules for the rest of the day."

"What?" Hannah blurted.

"Nem, sayidi." The door closed.

"I didn't think—I wasn't—" She cut herself off, unable to form words as Akin stood and held out his hand to her. The heat in his eyes made her throat go dry. "Right *now*?"

"I don't intend to seduce you here," he drawled. "Not this time, anyway. Not our first time. But I've been thinking about this long enough that if I have to spend the day in a state of anticipation, I'm liable to last about five minutes when we get to the good part. Come."

CHAPTER TEN

SHE NERVOUSLY PUT her hand in his and he drew her to her feet. Then he kissed her, just once, and her heart raced as he smiled conspiratorially, as though they shared a secret.

They did, as it happened. He used his thumbprint to unlock a door and showed her into a private passage, which took them past an unmarked door that she vaguely suspected was the throne room. She got turned around after that. They passed an emergency exit and went up and down a few flights of stairs. He had to use his thumb on three more doors, or they would have been trapped in dead ends. She didn't see one camera.

"You're not lost, are you?"

He sent her such a pithy look she chuckled away her nerves.

"I had to ask. We're going to need a tent and campfire soon."

"This is why I don't commute this way. I had these security doors put in place myself so I have no one else to blame, but these passages had ceased to provide the privacy they were designed for. When I was a child, Eijaz and I played hide-and-seek for hours here, but servants began using them as a shortcut. Doors were being left unlocked and propped open. Today, however, they allow me to steal my wife to my own chamber, with no one the wiser."

He touched a final sensor and a wooden panel swung inward, revealing that this particular entrance was disguised by a bookshelf inside his den.

"Almost no one," he corrected as a bearded man in a white tunic and plain cotton pants appeared in the doorway, a surprised look on his face. "My butler, Ulama. The Princess and I do not wish to be disturbed."

"Unless the baby needs me," Hannah added as the man dipped his skullcap-covered head in a bow and evaporated.

"He will need me, you know." Not for a while and it might be time to see if he would take a bottle, but she would make that decision when her phone buzzed.

For the moment she was fascinated to be in her husband's private space. Like his office, this place didn't have a lot of froufrou touches, but the soothing colors made it a place of retreat. He had windows looking out into the real world, not just the courtyard, which briefly distracted her.

"You don't have a dining room," she noted. Only a table in a nook that offered a view of the desert. She and he shared a chef, though. She knew that much.

"I don't entertain. You have the dining room and the bigger lounge for hosting family gatherings. Everything else is hosted in the formal rooms of the palace."

She would have dismissed this as a bachelor's apartment, but when they arrived in his bedroom, she saw that it was even bigger and more sumptuous than her own. He had a massive bed and a full sitting room with a window overlooking the pool area. There was also a screen of greenery, but she still had a moment of shyness when he stood behind her, clasped her shoulders and kissed her neck.

"What's wrong?" he asked, lifting his mouth as he sensed her tension.

"What if Nura can see us?"

He moved away to touch a button on the wall. Bone-colored drapes whispered from the corners to cover the glass while the room remained softly lit.

"Don't you have blackout blinds so you can sleep if you have to?"

"Yes. But I want to see you."

She shook her head in automatic rejection, linking her hands nervously as he came back to her. "I don't want that."

"No? Then how will I see this dimple of yours?" He tilted up her face and set his thumb in the middle of her chin. "It appears when you're digging in your heels. It frustrates the hell out of me, but it's so damned cute I always want to kiss it."

He was barely moving his thumb, but it felt like the most erotic caress. The heat in his eyes scrambled her brain.

"I want to make love, Akin, I do." She heard the plaintive note in her voice and hated herself for being so insecure. "But I have a lot of hang-ups about sex. I never felt attractive or like anyone really wanted m-me." Her lips trembled despite how hard she fought to speak evenly. "I know that no one is perfect, and you don't expect *me* to be perfect, but I'm still really scared that I'll disappoint you, either in the way I look or my lack of experience…" She shrugged to encompass all the many ways she could fail to measure up.

He didn't laugh or dismiss her. His dark brows quirked with concern. "I've been nothing but satisfied and delighted every time I've held you. I hope you know that. I hope you've felt the same?"

"Of course, but that was only fooling around. I got to keep my clothes on."

His mouth pursed in thought, then his hand moved to her neck. "Let's try this."

He unwound the silk scarf she had draped over her hair this morning. It tickled her nape as he gently slithered it free. He made a band of it in front of her eyes and started to tie it over them.

"Wait! No. *You* should wear the blindfold," she protested, catching at his strong wrist.

"I'm the one who wants to see, *ya amar.* You're the one who doesn't want to see my reaction. You'll feel it, though. I promise you won't have any doubt how desirable I find you."

He waited a beat, then stepped closer so he could see behind her head. He smoothed her hair out of the way before he tied the scarf in place. When he dropped his hands, they lightly traced her spine, drawing her into him so she could feel he was already aroused.

"Feel how irresistible you are to me? Do you hear it?" His voice was husked in a way that seemed to abrade her all over, sensitizing her skin. His hot breath grazed her cheek before his lips nuzzled across her skin, seeking her ear. "These are not my earrings."

"No." She started to bring her hand up to the sleeper hoops she'd let Nura poke in when she pierced her lobes. They had stung for about five minutes, leaving her to wonder why she'd been so scared for so long.

Her hand bumped into his arm. She let

her touch rest against his ribs, disconcerted by the fact she couldn't see. It was silly. She mostly closed her eyes when they kissed anyway, but this was different. She *couldn't* open them. It was like making love in the absolute dark and it emboldened her to let her hands explore where her eyes couldn't, trying to get her bearings that way.

He made a noise of satisfaction and his mouth trailed to capture hers. Here, when he kissed her with this depth of passion, everything was right in her world. They kissed like that for long minutes, exactly as they had on other occasions, hands whispering over linen and charmeuse, slipping free a button or delving beneath an edge to find warm skin.

Except, rather than fondling under her blouse, he opened it completely and brushed it off her shoulders. Rather than lifting her skirt, he unzipped it and dropped it to the floor. And rather than hug her close, he stepped back so there was nothing but cool air around her.

"Akin," she protested, automatically shielding herself with her arms.

"Oh, no, *ya amar*." He took her hands and held them out to her sides like wings. "You are far too modest if you think that what I am seeing is anything less than perfection."

"That's not true." She wore low-heeled sandals that were pretty enough. All her clothes came from top-end designers now, but despite lace panels and jewel tones, her underwear was still the least sexy style. Thongs and cheekies were way too uncomfortable, so she wore high-waisted, maximum-coverage panties. And she was wearing a nursing bra, for heaven's sake.

"How does this come off?" he asked, touching once between her breasts before stepping to follow the bra to its clasp below her shoulder blades.

"Akin." She tried to be brave, she really did. He was her husband, she wanted to make love with him, and he would see her naked eventually, but she felt so *vulnerable*. When he dropped the bra away and stepped back again, she curled her arms to hide her breasts.

"Hannah." His voice was that commanding tone, but there was a catch in it. Just enough that she didn't take umbrage. In fact, her nipples hardened against the press of her own arms. When he took her wrists and set kisses in each of her palms, tingles spread from her nape into her shoulders and down her whole body, weakening her knees and making them shake.

"If these hands continue to get in my way, I'll have to tie them behind you." He crossed her wrists behind her. "Keep them there. Pretend you have no choice but to let me see as much of you as I wish."

"That's kinky," she accused.

"Only if it excites you. Does it?" His hot hands gathered her breasts, gently plumping them. She could tell by the heat of his closeness and the angle of his breath that he was staring at the pale globes laced with fine blue lines. He was watching his own thumbs make circles around her distended nipples.

She shifted restlessly, thought about breaking her invisible bonds, but it was a little bit exciting to pretend she couldn't. A little bit freeing to imagine he had tied her up so she would be at his mercy.

"I think it does excite you." He sounded

pleased. "Your panting is making your breasts shake in my hands. It's the most beautiful sight I've ever seen."

"It's fear," she lied. "I'm being held hostage, if you recall."

"Oh, I am well aware. You are completely mine to touch and admire. If I wish to slide these down just a little…" His thumbs caught in the band of her panties and took them down so they cut low across her hips, exposing the fine hairs at the top of her mound. "Then I may do so. I can do anything I want to you and you are utterly helpless."

As she stood there trembling in a strange, erotic excitement, deeply aware of how exposed she was, his fingertips traced the line of elastic from hip to hip, pausing in the middle to pet and discover, ever so briefly, the place where her folds began to part.

Heat flooded up to her hairline and down to her loins. She was aware of a rush of damp arousal into silk and grew more and more sensitized, and more and more frustrated, as he continued to caress her with such teasing lightness.

"You are so lovely." His voice was guttural and rough while his touch stayed light.

"You're enjoying this," she accused, scandalized by how much he seemed to be embracing their fantasy.

"Believe it. It's all I can do not to bend you over the foot of my bed." He drew her into a hot kiss, pressing her naked body into the hot linen that still covered him.

She almost forgot she was "bound," but he loosely grappled her wrists in one of his hands while the other slid beneath her lowered panties to cup her backside.

He seemed to love her bottom. He never missed an opportunity to touch her like this when they kissed, stroking in a way that made her squirm against him, then firming to press her mound into his shape.

Today he traced the line between her cheeks, slowly, slowly easing her panties down until they were fully off her butt and cutting across the backs of her thighs. Then he drew back again and his hand gave her wrists a reminding squeeze before he said, "Are we coming up to Valentine's Day? Because I have a gift to finish unwrapping."

She heard his knee click as he crouched before her to take the lace and silk all the way to her ankles. Her elbows twitched as she fought her invisible cuffs. She clenched her eyes behind her blindfold, unsteady on her feet as he lifted them one by one to remove her sandals.

He rose with another click of his knee and she heard all the clothes being flung away from around her feet. He touched her hip to shuffle her a few steps, perhaps moving her closer to the bed. She heard him remove his clothes and licked her lips, waiting, but there was only silence now.

"What are you doing?"

"Looking at you." His voice was behind her. "You're in front of a mirror so I can see everything, Hannah. Your round ass and lush breasts and pale thighs and soft stomach. Your obedience." He touched her crossed wrists.

She had started to draw them apart, but firmed their cross, releasing a small whimper of helpless frustration as she did.

"I'm looking at that mouth going all flat with annoyance and thinking about how much pleasure you give me with it. So much, I can hardly speak. I'm looking at your hair." He touched where it stopped at her nape. "So soft I want to sleep with my cheek on it."

He stepped up behind her, so his hot frame brushed her back and pinned her crossed wrists between his hard abdomen and her lower back. His thick sex rested against her buttocks, hot and heavy, while his hand came around her. His fingertip offered a barely-there caress along the seam of her folds.

"I'm looking at the dampness here that tells me you're aroused," he said huskily against her ear. "I feel so impatient to have you, I'm shaking with it. Do not ever let me hear again that you're anything but beautiful, Hannah. That is an order."

She might have had an intelligent response if he hadn't chosen that second to sink his touch into her damp folds and gently part her. She stumbled back into him and he caught her close, pinning her arms even more firmly so she was trapped as he sought her swollen bud and encircled, gliding his touch over and around and across.

Intense pleasure was jolting through her.

White light flashed behind her eyes. Her knees nearly gave out on her.

"Akin," she gasped, hanging in his arms.

"Poor little captive, so helpless. Let's tie you to the bed." He removed his intimate touch and steadied her. She could have wept; her sense of loss was so profound.

Moments later, cool sheets were at her back and he was guiding her hands above her head.

She scrabbled ineffectual nails against the quilted leather of his headboard while his cropped beard tickled her chin and throat and between her breasts. Her stomach muscles contracted as he arrived there, and she realized where he was going. She pressed her thighs together. "You don't have to do that."

"You are correct. I am in absolute control of everything that happens here. I may do whatever I want, *ya amar*. Do I have to tie your legs open?" He used effortless strength to part her thighs, but she was shaking more than resisting.

"You're a barbarian at heart, aren't you?" But she pretended her legs were bound, as well. She could do nothing but let him have his way with her. It was titillating to believe but liberating in how it allowed her to accept his caresses without guilt that she was being selfish. Without fear that she didn't deserve to be pleasured and worshipped this way.

"I will be satisfied with nothing less than your complete surrender." He was looking at her; she knew he was. Delicately parting her and letting his hot breath waft across her sensitive flesh as he spoke.

The anticipation was so palpable she was ready to scream with frustration.

"You are magnificent, Hannah. Feel it. Believe it."

He claimed her, stealing across intimate territory with his lips and tongue. He undermined her resistance and staked a claim, easing two fingers inside her.

She writhed with pleasure. She could have broken her pretend bonds and reached for him. She could have torn off her blindfold and made this a more mutual act, but as much as she wanted to give him pleasure, she wanted to give him *her*. He wanted her unequivocally. Why else would he pleasure her like this?

With that realization, she understood that whatever had held her back in the past might have been real, but there were no shackles today except the ones she allowed herself to believe in.

She let go of her old hurts once and for all. She didn't worry how she looked to him, only that he knew how magnificent he made her feel. She abandoned herself to the agonizing joy he was bestowing on her, holding her body open to him while holding back none of her moans and sobs of pleasure. She cried out his name again and again. When her climax hit, she held herself taut, hips lifted in offering, absent of inhibition as she exalted in his unrelenting ministrations.

As she panted in reaction and her flesh sang and her abdomen shook with reaction, his hands roamed from her thighs to her breasts. His mouth followed, taking restrained bites from her stomach and the inner swells of her heavy breasts and he sucked a decided mark against her neck.

Then he shifted so he was aligned with her

entrance and brushed the blindfold off her eyes. Here was the barbarian, eyes glittering, cheekbones sharp as knives, the weight and strength of him caging her.

"You're mine," he said in a rasping voice laden with passion as he slowly, inexorably pressed into her.

She wouldn't dream of arguing and couldn't speak anyway. The sensation as he filled her was too intense. She abandoned her invisible restraints and closed her arms and legs around him. Claimed him as hers. She wouldn't entertain any other belief as they kissed and he sank fully into her, so hard, so hot. So deeply a part of her that it was unescapable and profound.

He gave an abbreviated thrust, watching as he did, testing her readiness.

She didn't shrink from his all-seeing gaze. She probably still wore the flush of her recent climax. Her eyelids were heavy, and her lips tingled. Everything about this moment was deeply intimate, but they were in it together. She drew his head down to kiss while pressing his shoulder with her other hand.

In an effortless twist, he hugged her tight

and rolled so she was on top. She smiled and caught his arms, finding his hands and pressing them to the mattress beside his head.

One dark eyebrow went up, then his gaze narrowed as she sat tall upon him, running her hands over her body as she began to un- dulate upon him.

"Vixen," he bit out.

"You unleashed the savage in me. You have no one to blame but yourself."

"Use me, then." He lifted his hips, encour- aging her to ride him. "Show me how much you want me."

She splayed her hands on his chest, brac- ing herself as they began to move together. It was raw and wild. Blatant and intense. Her breasts jiggled and their bodies slapped. When her thighs tired, he clamped his hands on her hips and guided her rhythm. She curled her fingers on his chest and thought she must be pulling his chest hair, but the tension was coiling in her and she was nearly there, as was he.

She bit her lip and watched him bare his teeth. She wanted to close her eyes as the wave began to engulf her, but she held his slitted gaze as dark color washed into his chest and face and the tendons in his neck stood up.

At the same time orgasm struck deep inside her, dragging a cry of repletion from her, he shouted and arched and let out his own shouts of release.

An unfamiliar intermittent hum woke Akin.

He dragged his eyes open to find his wife in one of his robes, leaning into pillows pressed against the headboard. She was nursing Qaswar, who was gulping loudly between humming in the way of anyone who was enjoying a hearty meal after a long fast.

"Is he always like that?"

"I don't know why I thought I could do this without waking you. He's like a starving wolf on a lamb, aren't you, my little glutton?" She tenderly stroked her son's hair. "Growling and gobbling."

"I don't mind." Akin absently reached for the boy's foot, which poked from his knee-length pajamas. It wasn't even as long as his thumb, and his small toes curled as Akin ran his finger into the boy's arch. He had the most ridiculous urge to press his cheek to the soft sole and let the baby feel the texture of his beard.

He released him and fell onto his back, curling his arm under his head, disturbed by how hard he'd slept, but damn, he felt good. Relaxed. He could get used to this, he thought, but immediately a cool draft entered his chest. A harsh recognition that nothing in life was permanent, so he shouldn't let himself get used to it. Even people who seemed to care could cause pain and disappear.

He realized Hannah was looking at him with a small frown. "Problem?" he asked.

"I just wondered…" She touched the baby's foot. "You said you and Eijaz used to play in the passageways. That makes me think you were friends, but… I know you said you didn't want to talk about your childhood. It's fine if you don't, but I always wished I had a sibling. I wondered if you think we'll ever give Qaswar brothers or sisters."

"Ambush me in my own bed when I'm too weak to walk away, why don't you?" he muttered, frowning to the ceiling.

He loathed dragging open heavy doors inside him, scraping across the grit of the past, but her expression was very naked and vulnerable. Their physical intimacy had formed a connection between them that was delicate and so tenuous it terrified him how easily it could be broken. He couldn't shut her down.

"We were friends. Very different because we were raised very differently. He was the future king and mentored for that role. Spoiled. So spoiled," he sighed. "But charming and likable, and I was his confidante, the only person who really understood the pressures he faced. The expectations he feared he couldn't meet. In that way, I sometimes think my parents did me a favor, making me work like hell for each tiny shred of approval. Like how the straight A students fall apart when they reach university, but the ones who are used to getting Cs already know how to dig in."

"I thought it was just your mother who was…less than forthcoming with her affection. But I don't understand how any parent can favor one child over another," she protested.

"My mother had a stillbirth after me, a daughter. Seeing how Eijaz's death devastated her gives me some indication how thoroughly the loss of my sister must have broken her. She had two sons, you see. If she had to give up one of her babies, her daughter should have been the one to survive."

Her arms tightened around Qaswar. "That's so wrong, Akin. I'm sorry she's lost two children, but no. That was deeply unfair of her. And you're here. That ought to count for something."

He didn't bother pointing out his mother's reduced mental capacities these days.

"I'm really sorry you lost your brother, though. He must have been your confidante, too? Did he never stand up for you against them?"

"In his way," he said on an exhale. "He told our father I was planning to elope."

"He *did* that?"

"He thought he was helping."

"You believe that?"

"I do." He'd been furious at the time, but it had been typical of Eijaz to do what he thought was best without thinking through to the consequences.

Akin watched her shift the baby to her shoulder and pat his back. The day he'd met her, he'd thought Eijaz must be laughing at the predicament he'd thrust Akin into, but now he wondered if any divine intervention might have had a more benevolent motive. The things he felt for Hannah were infinitely deeper and more complex than that youthful crush he'd once entertained. Had his brother tried to repair that long-ago injury from beyond his grave?

"Do you want more children?" he asked her.

"Not today," she said with a wryly slanted glance. "But I will." Her nod held calm certainty. "I thought when I got pregnant that one would be enough, but now I want someone for Qaswar to play hide-and-seek with. I want a family." She knitted her brow anxiously. "I want *this*."

She shifted to set the baby on the mattress between them and slid down to face him across the wriggling little boy.

"I want to make love and tell each other

things no one else knows, and I want us to play with our children." She held a hand against Qaswar's foot so he could work his tiny leg muscles against it.

"Children don't stay children," Akin warned. "Happy moments are only moments. Everything changes eventually. You know that, don't you?" It was a harsh reality that had been drilled so deeply into him he couldn't see outside it.

"Sometimes things change for the better. A baby can grow up strong and capable of handling the challenges he faces. A life alone can turn into one with…a partner." The emotion in her eyes grew even more undisguised.

He withdrew slightly. She didn't understand the risk she was taking in opening her heart that much. Hurt became inevitable and he would do anything to keep her from being hurt.

Not that he wanted to yank that trusting innocence away from her when they were tucked so safely into a rare pocket of contentment. Hell, there was a part of him that longed for partnership and family and belief in the future, too.

But he wasn't a fool. He didn't *ask* for disappointment and loss and pain.

He dropped his gaze to Qaswar.

The baby cycled his legs and his abstract gaze moved aimlessly then snagged on Akin's. His tiny mouth stretched in a smile so much like his brother's it kicked Akin straight in the heart.

It was such a powerful moment it shook Akin to the core. Hannah and Qaswar were already rattling the gates of his heart, threatening to make him even more vulnerable than he was.

"I've only ever protected what everyone else has, Hannah. I don't know how to imagine more for myself, let alone make it a reality. Maybe…" He stopped himself, embarrassed.

"What?" she prompted.

"I don't know. I can't help thinking it will be different after the ceremony. Once my father recognizes me as— Not his heir, obviously, but his temporary successor at least. Something more than…" He peeked down into the basement of his soul. "More than a second son. That's been a stain. I would never condemn my own child to that position."

"No, you wouldn't." She set her hand on his cheek. "*I* wouldn't."

He wanted to believe that, but there was a part of him that refused to see and want and accept that he deserved the life she described. If he let himself yearn for it, any ultimate denial would destroy him.

"My life does not get reshaped by a happiness list," he said gently, cushioning his words by holding on to the hand she tried to draw back. He moved it from his bearded cheek so he could kiss her palm. "I admire you so much for going after what you want out of life. I want to give you everything you could ever desire, but can we talk about more children another time?"

She bit her lip in hurt but nodded. "Of course."

CHAPTER ELEVEN

I WANT YOUR HEART. That was what Hannah had wanted to say.

Ironically, the one thing she had purposely left off her happiness list was anything to do with winning the love of a man, yet here she was with pretty much the whole list achieved and she wasn't happy.

She couldn't resent Akin for holding back, though. She understood how his parents had taught him not to trust that he was as entitled as anyone else to a fulfilling life. She also understood how hard it was to decide what personal happiness looked like and go after it.

The worst part was, she couldn't change his mind for him. All she could do was believe that time would heal all wounds and try to give him that time. At least she had the reassurance of his physical attentions. They made love every chance they got, which was pure magic, but she didn't realize how completely he wanted to share a bed until he showed up in her room in the middle of the night, sounding quite annoyed.

"Why didn't you come back?"

"Qaswar took forever to settle. I didn't want to wake you," she murmured drowsily as he joined her in her own bed and dragged her into the spoon of his body.

"I was lying awake worried something was wrong. We're changing wings after the coronation, so this won't happen again."

He made it sound like a dire warning, but it made her smile with gladness in the dark before she drifted back to sleep.

The coronation was only a few weeks away and final plans were falling into place. Akin had approved all her arrangements and offered special praise for her attention to detail—as if she'd never had to organize a faculty lunch that satisfied vegan, kosher and nut allergy requests in the same meal plan before.

Hannah was in the middle of a meeting that would put the final touches on the celebration when her assistant touched her elbow and whispered she had an urgent call from her husband.

"My father passed," Akin said abruptly. "I've just informed my mother. I have to make more calls. Can you bring the baby and sit with her? She's asking for him."

"Of course. I'm so sorry, Akin."

He said something noncommittal and hung up.

A cold premonition entered her heart. She didn't make any announcements to the staff, unsure if it was her place, only hurriedly called the nanny to meet her in the Queen's chambers. But the whole while, she was thinking about what he'd said that day about how the coronation would change things. That if his father recognized him, he would start to feel accepted as something more than a stain.

The next days were difficult, as all such losses were. She barely saw her husband except when she stood beside him to greet visitors who came to pay their respects. It was an endless procession of long faces and hushed voices. Between that were spells of placating his mother and reminding her that her husband was gone. The Queen had taken a very hard turn with the loss.

Hannah also had to call off the coronation. Instead, the day after the King's funeral, they were visited by the representatives from parliament. If Akin had been sleeping, it hadn't been with her. He looked like hell.

"By unanimous vote, we have cemented your authority as Regent of Baaqi until our Crown Prince is ready to assume his duties," one of the men said—or so it was translated quietly into Hannah's ear.

The formality lasted ten minutes. They took their leave and Hannah finally had a moment alone with her husband. He looked so drawn, with his hollow cheeks and bruised eyes, that she reached for him.

"Is that really all that was required? I thought the coronation was meant to prove… something." She shrugged ineffectually.

"It was." Akin's voice was empty of emotion. His arm was cold and unresponsive. "It would have proved my father wanted me to have the appointment. That he trusted me and recognized me as his surviving son and a competent leader. It was pure vanity on my part," he added in a bitter scoff at himself.

"Don't say that." His despair broke her heart. "It's okay that you wanted his recognition. That's not vanity. That's being human."

"Wanting love as a child is natural. Wanting it as an adult is immature and self-indulgent."

"No, it's not! *I* want love. Everyone does." Anxiety clawed at her along with inner warnings that he was in too much pain to hear through it, but she kept speaking. "I'm sorry your parents withheld their love for you. You deserve it and I know it's no substitute, but… I love you." It hurt to say it the way it might hurt to pull her own heart out of her chest and show it to him, but she offered it to him all the same.

He sucked in a pained breath, not moving, but visibly withdrawing from her.

Don't, she silently protested.

"Hannah, I can't… I told you I would give you everything I could, but that life you want? It's not in my power to give you that." His eyes and voice were bleak. "I'm not the man who can make that happen for you."

How do you know if you haven't tried? That was what she wanted to say.

"I'm not going to stop wanting it, Akin. Who will give it to me if not you? Am I supposed to find it with someone else? Or just accept a life that falls short of..." She couldn't disparage the life she had. The son she'd been given. The life he had already given her.

But she was greedy. She wanted more. And she couldn't imagine being with anyone else, not when she loved Akin with everything in her.

"Yes," he said distantly. "Find someone else." He walked away.

CHAPTER TWELVE

HANNAH WAS DEVASTATED, but she let him go because he was obviously in too much pain to be rational.

He didn't just walk away, though. He *left*.

It took her two days to realize it, but she finally ran the gamut of his assistants to reach his top aide. "He went into the desert. I didn't realize you didn't know, or I would have informed you myself," the man apologized.

"What does that mean? Like…where in the desert? For how long? Why?" How could she possible reach him there? Was she supposed to not even *try*? Her desolation was so profound it was a type of grief.

"That is very hard to answer," the aide said with remorse. "I can make enquiries. It may take some time."

"Thank you." Hannah walked out, crushed,

but more than that, she was *mad*. Maybe Akin had never promised to love her, but he had promised to treat her with respect. Maybe he hadn't promised to make her happy, but he wasn't allowed to hurt her. Not on purpose.

While an old, fragile part of her wanted to crawl away and hide from the pain of his abandonment, she let her anger at him fuel her. Maybe she was kidding herself, pretending it was pique, not a broken heart that had her make her own inquiries, but it was safer than believing she was foolishly chasing a man who didn't really want her.

She deserved better than this, she told herself and made herself believe it as she texted Galila for advice.

Do I let him grieve in his own way? Will he be angry if I go after him?

Galila was not only intimately connected to the nomad families who traversed the deserts, she understood best the sort of man she was dealing with. Her response helped Hannah decide on her next course of action.

Probably. Men like ours are too proud to lean on a woman if they can avoid it. But if he's hurting and you love him, be there for him anyway.

Galila arranged a helicopter herself.

Which was how Hannah got to the oasis ahead of him.

The sizable pool was a jewel of blue in an ocean of sand that charmed her immediately. A small tribe was in residence. Hannah and her entourage of bodyguards and nannies, cooks and maids were greeted warily until they realized Qaswar was with her. Then the entire mood became celebratory, and they were all welcomed warmly.

Hannah wondered if Akin would welcome the sight of her. He would likely be furious, while her own anger had dissipated into uncertainty. Had she really come all this way to be rejected? Again?

She had to wait two full days to find out. It was nerve-racking but pleasant to be out of the palace. The nomads were happy to educate her on native plants and their culture, and help her practice her rudimentary Arabic.

She was in the middle of learning a traditional lullaby when a thundering commotion and a huge dust cloud appeared at the edge of the bowl that surrounded the oasis. A half dozen camels bawled as they were galloped down the slope into the encampment.

It would have been terrifying if Hannah hadn't recognized the tall bearing of her husband within seconds. Elemental and dynamic, he took her breath with his imposing presence. She handed Qaswar to a nanny and met him as he dismounted.

"What happened? Is the baby okay?" He was covered in dust and sand.

"He's perfectly fine. Smothered nearly to death by all the adoring arms who want to hold him." She glanced toward the tent where Qaswar was being put down for a nap in the shade, a dozen minders hovering nearby.

"Then what brought you here? My heart stopped when the hawkers told me you had been here two days, waiting for me."

"Where am I supposed to be?" she asked

with a flash of the anger that was the only thing she'd been letting herself feel. "If not with my husband. What are *you* doing here?"

"You did not come all the way out here to ask me that." The thunderous look he gave her nearly made her back up a step, even though there was a flash of something behind his outrage that she couldn't interpret.

"I did." She held her ground, but it felt as though she stood on insubstantial dunes that shifted beneath her feet. "Was I supposed to wait back at the palace for you until you returned to inform me what sort of future I could expect? Live whatever pale, useless life you told me to live?"

His expression didn't change.

The sand was slipping away beneath her, and now she felt like she was sliding through an hourglass.

"I love you, Akin. I told you that. And even though you were in a lot of pain when I said it the first time, your reaction left a lot to be desired. Think long and hard about how you react today."

The lift of her chin was pure bravado, because inside, she shook worse than she ever had during one of their confrontations. Those other times, she hadn't had nearly so much of herself invested. Before she'd felt his touch and his lips and shared secrets across a pillow, she would have been able to bear his anger and rejection. But now she loved him and that was her heart right there on the sand. If he kicked it away this time, he would do irrevocable damage to the fragile bond between them.

He said nothing. He stood there coated in dust, nostrils flared, eyes going black as his pupils expanded.

Inexplicably, her heart began to pound in panic. She swallowed and started to lean onto her back foot, sensing real danger.

Before she could whirl and run, he swooped and caught her and swung her over his shoulder. It happened so fast her nose was in the back of his dusty robe before she realized what he intended.

He barked something in Arabic and she heard someone answer him, but she couldn't tell who or what they said, or even where he was taking her.

"What are you doing?" she cried, wriggling enough to test his grip, but also hanging on because he was starting to walk.

"This is who I am, Hannah. You say you love me, but you've only ever seen my civilized side, when I've been trying to run a country and earn my parents' respect and keep from scaring the sexually repressed librarian."

"I'm not sexually repressed."

The cadence of his steps slowed as he began wading into the water.

"What are you *doing*?" She kicked her feet, pretty sure he'd lost his mind.

"I'm filthy." He swept her around so she dropped into the cradle of his arms and her startled eyes were even with his. "And I'm furious. I would have settled for my father telling me I was doing right by my nephew. I would have settled for my mother calling you my wife, not the nanny. I was furious that I let you see how much those things meant to me and how little I meant to them. I was hurt and angry and worst of all—"

His mouth flattened.

"I was furious that I couldn't see myself giving you the thing you want most. I don't know how to make someone else happy, Hannah. I've never *been* happy."

Not even with her? A little? Her heart clutched in agony.

"So when you asked if you should find the life you want with someone else, I thought, yes. She deserves it even if I can't give it to her. And I did what I've always done. I went into the desert, where life is pared down to the basics of survival. Where the things I want, the things I *need*, are purely physical. Those are needs I can meet myself. But you have *ruined* that for me, Hannah. The whole time I've been out here, all I could think was how stupid I was to have left you. So I'm furious with you, too."

He threw her.

She screamed and flailed and remembered to catch her breath at the last second, right before she hit the water in a giant splash and plunge into its blessed, silent chill.

When she came up and toed to find the bottom, she was up to her breasts in the water, her abaya tangled around her.

He stood with the water at his waist, dragging at his clothes and throwing them toward the shore.

Beyond him, she saw that he'd managed to clear the area. Flaps had been pulled down on tents and voices were drifting in retreat as the camels were drawn away to the corral set on the far side of a dune. Not a single pair of eyes so much as peeked from behind a dangling bit of washing on a line.

"I'm not going to leave my son to go looking for some other man. Did you think about him at all? Because this is your chance to be a better father than—"

"I'm already a better father than the one I had," he snapped. "And I do want more children, for your information. Not because I want one that's 'mine,' either. Qaswar *is* mine in the ways that count. But I want that far-fetched dream of yours where we make love and play with our children and get through the bad times on the belief that they don't last. That good times will come again."

"Is that belief really so far-fetched?" she cried, hurt that he sounded so disparaging.

He sobered. "Being out here was bad,

Hannah. It was nothing but loss and a feeling that sat like a sick pile of rocks in my gut, that I'd thrown away my soul by leaving you. That what we had was gone forever and it was my own fault that I was suffering."

"So why didn't you come back to fight for me? *Us?*" That hurt. It cut so deeply she could hardly breathe.

"I didn't get the chance, did I?" he said gently. "Because here you are. Proving that the good shows up, whether I know how to accept it or not. Finding you here is good, Hannah. Seeing you when I was feeling like hell is *good.* I shouldn't have left without speaking to you. I shouldn't have shut you out when letting you in is like...turning on a light inside myself. Like setting down the heaviest weight. Like sinking into cool, clear water when I'm hot and sweaty and filthy." He waded in toward her. "I don't understand why you would be this good to me, but you are. I won't throw you away again."

They were ignoring the part where he'd thrown her into this pool, she presumed, but she was beginning to tentatively hope.

"You're on my list," she said with a lift

of her shoulder. "Even when you're sweaty and grouchy and uncivilized, you make me happy, so I had to come after you."

Tender agony clenched across his grimy face for one moment, the way emotion overpowered him sometimes when he didn't seem to know what to make of her.

"Even though I'm liable to be that way often?" He splashed the dust from his face. "I've thought about making my own list, you know. But you're the whole thing. What else could I need?"

"Akin." She dipped her chin, blinking more than water from her lashes.

"Why aren't you keeping up, *ya amar*?" He nodded at the clothes she still wore. "Too angry? I've hurt you too much?"

Her hurt and anger were dissolving beneath the emotions he was making no effort to disguise. In fact, the gleam in his gaze was so intense she wound up shyly looking down to unzip the garment, trying to escape how monumental it felt to be the subject of that much admiration and value and regard. Something inside her was growing too big for her skin to contain it. Her throat ached in a good way.

"My top is white," she said huskily as she let the abaya float away. She was using levity to keep herself from dissolving into emotive tears. "We could hold that wet T-shirt contest we talked about last Christmas."

A brief pulse of surprise, then he said, "Let me see," and drew her to him.

She was so buoyant it took no effort for him to draw her up so she could wrap her legs around his waist and reveal her soaked torso.

"It's not ideal," she murmured. Her nursing bra was clearly visible.

"It's a preliminary round," he allowed. "But you're definitely on the way to the finals."

"We could hold another qualifying contest later," she suggested, linking her hands behind his neck. *In the future*, she intimated. The one they would have. Together.

His gaze stayed on her chest. "A tournament circuit. I like that idea."

"Despite the lack of competition, I believe

I have a shot at the title. One of the judges seems very biased in my favor."

"The *only* judge," he said in stern warning, "is extremely biased. He also has an uncanny ability to spot excellence. Eleven out of ten. Without the bra, your score will triple."

"Hey." She cupped the sides of his face. "My eyes are up here."

"You started it." He made no effort to disguise the lust simmering behind his love.

"I think I fell in love with you the first time you made a joke. Do you know that?"

"I have never made a joke in my life. I am always completely serious," he assured her.

She gathered all her courage, even though this gamble wasn't nearly as frightening as she had always feared. Happiness was right here. All she had to do was grab it.

"Do you love me, Akin?"

"I love you so much I cannot breathe, Hannah. I am terrified that something will happen to you, because I do not know how to face life without you anymore. But I am so glad to have you by my side. In my arms. In my head and in my heart."

Her mouth trembled and her throat could only manage a thready whisper. "That is a much better reaction than the first time. For the record."

"For the record, there is no contest. You are the most beautiful, perfect woman ever created. But as beautiful as you are, especially in the throes of passion, I am going to make love to you in your tent. Your body is very much my vision to enjoy and no one else's."

"So possessive," she teased, secretly delighted.

"Believe it."

A few minutes later, when their damp, naked bodies were coming together on the cushion-strewn bed in her tent, he paused to take in her pale curves. His reverent hand stroked the back of her shoulder, down her back and waist and hips to her bottom and her thigh.

"You really are the most beautiful, perfect woman," he murmured worshipfully.

And she believed him.

EPILOGUE

"EXPLAIN THAT AGAIN." Qaswar might only be seven years old, but his dark brows were perfectly capable of a thunderous frown of astonishment.

Akin loved him so much his chest could barely contain it sometimes. His son-slash-nephew had so many of Eijaz's physical traits it was unquestionable whose son he was. He also had Eijaz's outgoing personality and idealistic vision of how the world should run. All of that was tempered with glimpses of Hannah that showed up in an expression of curiosity or an incisive way of seeing things or a quiet moment of compassion.

Not that Qaswar was in any mood to hear about his inherited traits today.

Akin glanced at his wife. She was biting her lips together as she closed the children's book that seemed to be prompting more questions than it answered.

"Which part is confusing you?" Akin asked. "Because you've always known that I'm actually your uncle." They had made that clear from a very early age in ways that had been appropriate at the time, pointing to other blended families as examples. "And we talked a little about where babies come from when your sister was born." That had been last year and Qaswar hadn't been that interested.

"Yes, but—" A dimple appeared in Qaswar's chin and he looked between them with disbelief. "You *do* that?"

Akin took Hannah's hand. "Yes." They special-hugged the hell out of each other as much as their busy schedules allowed.

"But I didn't do that with your biological father," Hannah clarified. "That's why I wanted you to read the book, so we could explain that part."

Qaswar had *not* been eager for a reading assignment when it wasn't a school day, particularly one on reproductive science that included illustrations of smiling sperm and ovum with eyelashes.

"This is information we wanted you to learn straight from us," Akin said. "We thought you were old enough to understand it, but we don't have to talk a lot about it right now if you don't want to. You can bring it up anytime in future, though. And when your brother and sister are old enough, we'll explain it to them, too."

Akin hadn't known it was possible to love this wide and hard, but he would have ten more children if Hannah was up for it, he loved his existing three so much.

"Okay but tell me again how the doctors just *mixed it up*," Qaswar said. "Because it's not like when the maid accidentally puts your socks away in your brother's drawer, is it? It seems like something that's pretty important. Shouldn't they have been more organized?"

"Yes," Akin assured him. "And I am not one to excuse incompetence, but in this case, I can't regret their lack of attention to detail. In fact, I think it was the best thing that could have happened for all of us."

Qaswar shook his head in bemusement. "I guess." In the next second, he had shrugged off one of the most profound, defining moments of his parents' lives. "*Now* will you play hide-and-seek with us?"

"Sure," Akin said dryly. "Go get Kamal." Akin had promised to take them into the passageways where they slipped out of sight around corners then leaped out to scare one another from their skins. He had to warn security when they were going in, because their shouts alarmed the staff who heard it through the walls, but his boys loved it, and Akin did, too.

Hannah sagged into him before he could rise. Her shoulders were shaking. He realized she was gasping for breath, she was laughing so hard.

"What—?"

"Am I the drawer?" she sputtered.

A crack of laughter left him. He hadn't heard it like that, but now he absorbed Qaswar's remark about the socks put away in the drawer and laughed so hard his eyes grew wet.

The boys came back and Kamal cocked

his head, his grin the most endearing replica of Hannah's cheekiest smile. "What's so funny?"

Akin was too weak to speak. He squeezed Hannah. She was wiping her eyes.

"We're just happy," she said around her lingering chuckles. "Very, very happy."

They were.

* * * * *

LET'S TALK
Romance

For exclusive extracts, competitions
and special offers, find us online:

 facebook.com/millsandboon

 @millsandboonuk

 @millsandboon

Or get in touch on 0844 844 1351*

For all the latest titles coming soon,
visit millsandboon.co.uk/nextmonth

*Calls cost 7p per minute plus your phone company's price per
minute access charge